Moira Cherrie

Daddy, What's a Bastard?

AUSTIN MACAULEY PUBLISHERS™
LONDON · CAMBRIDGE · NEW YORK · SHARJAH

A CIP catalogue record for this title is available from the British Library.

ISBN 9781788234542 (Paperback)
ISBN 9781788234559 (E-Book)
www.austinmacauley.com

First Published (2018)
Austin Macauley Publishers Ltd™
25 Canada Square
Canary Wharf
London
E14 5LQ

Acknowledgements

No commendation is too high for the tireless and loving devotion of my friend, Betty Robinson, who typed my novel from a tatty manuscript and coped with the many changes with endless patience and without complaint.

Author's Note

This book was written forty years ago in a competition run by a well-known publishing firm. Despite winning first place, the book was not accepted for publication. Deeply disappointed and fearful of a second rejection, the author did not submit it elsewhere and it was laid aside and forgotten.

Some years later, the author re-appraised the work and submitted it to Austin Macauley Publishers with only a few alterations and a new title.

Because of the time gap between writing and publishing, it should be remembered that the author was recalling a time when social attitudes and relationships were different to those prevalent today.

Table of Contents

Chapter I
The Hockey Match

Jane sat huddled over her typewriter at the living room table, her grey top-hose legs swinging from the leather-bottomed chair, her laced-up shoes just failing to reach the floor. Her knees were rough and red from exposure to winter winds and the strands of wool at the right heel were beginning to thin out. Her school tie was sidling out of position, the maroon girdle of her gym tunic had long since lost its original, starched freshness, and there was a tell-tale stain on the bodice of the tunic where she had spilled her custard the previous week. Her hair was so straight it might have come off the ironing-board and, with middle shed and fringe vied for plainness with that of the flat-footed nomads painted on the tombs of ancient Egypt.

The typewriter was a heavy old-fashioned upright which her father had acquired at a nominal figure in his youth for business purposes. For Jane, it had been a plaything, and over the years she had developed an individual technique with which she covered the keyboard with intense deliberation and reasonable accuracy. Letters to a pen pal, verses, jokes and riddles were confided to its keys. Only occasionally was the narrative interrupted by a vulgar fraction or a percentage sign.

At thirteen, Jane was beginning to grow up. The child who had been something of a hoyden entered upon a new phase and life began in earnest, or so it seemed. The Three R's of the Primary School gave way to a multiplicity of new subjects. The class teacher who was followed and obeyed merely because she was there was succeeded by a train of queenly school-mistresses, each omniscient in her own subject. Suddenly, Jane began to do her schoolwork because she wanted to, fascinated equally by the unknown 'x' and the charms of the youthful Miss Jackson, the Maths teacher; by Latin verbs and the dignified but kindly Miss Kelvin; by the majestic sweep of Shakespeare and by Miss Chalmers who had introduced the class to his works. She found her life bounded on all sides by the ivy-covered school walls and she was happy.

The beat of the typewriter, as regular as the plodding steps of a Clydesdale horse, came to a sudden stop. Jane frowned. She was searching for a word, the right word, "le mot juste" as Miss Mason, the French teacher, would have said. The page in front of her was headed: "One of My Happiest Moments". In single-spaced typing which covered the page like a wall-to-wall carpet, unrelieved by a single paragraph inset, followed a dense, tense account of an unexpected encounter between Jane and Miss Chalmers that very Saturday afternoon:

...It was early spring but as mild as late April. The sky presented an unruffled front of blue and, on an impulse, Jane had set out on her bicycle in the direction of the school.

Weekends were sometimes rather dull. There was nothing to do at home, and though she did not suppose that there would be any activity at school she was drawn towards it as by a magnet.

How much she had worshipped Miss Jackson only her friends, Madge and Fiona, knew, but Jane sometimes wondered if they had really shared the intensity of her emotions. Madge had certainly looked rather misty-eyed when Miss Jackson had recently praised her neat equations and Fiona had enjoyed making both of them jealous when Miss Jackson had brought her down to the front near her own desk because she had been unable to see the board. But had *their* knees turned to water, as hers had, when Miss Jackson had passed them unexpectedly on the way to school the other morning and greeted them in friendly fashion? She wondered.

But then there was Miss Chalmers who recited the old Scots Ballads so enchantingly and who, though less attractive in Jane's eyes than Miss Jackson, had a smile that seemed to indicate an all-knowing mind and to radiate an all-embracing warmth. She had to brake suddenly as she realised that the approaching traffic lights were showing red. Could it be that she was forsaking Miss Jackson in favour of Miss Chalmers?

She cycled past the school playing-field which was opposite the school. A match was in progress and she dismounted to watch, rather puzzled, as the school elevens usually played in the mornings only. Moreover, the school stocking colour was maroon whereas the two teams now playing wore royal blue and green stockings respectively.

Suddenly, Jane's heart began to race. The blue-legged team was identified as the Earlswood District Eleven of which Miss Chalmers was Captain and which had the joint use of the school playing-field and facilities. Yes, there she was at the bully-off with that fascinating little bit of stick-play that Jane loved to watch. There she was running nimbly up-field, having passed the ball to a wing. The blue-legged forwards advanced sharing the ball among themselves, but the struggle was mostly in the area of the visiting team's goal. Play was brisk but not one of the players was half so excited as the lone supporter of the home team who peeped enthralled through the fence.

Goal for the home team! And it was Miss Chalmers who had shot it! Jane grasped the fence till her knuckles showed white. Glory, glory for Miss Chalmers! Glory for the royal blue legs which had been everywhere at once. Glory, hallelujah, that anyone so beautiful, so wonderful as Miss Chalmers had ever walked on the face of the earth or raced down a hockey pitch! Yes, she *was* beautiful, Jane could see that now. Every bit as beautiful as Miss Jackson, perhaps more so. She had moosie broon hair with a lovely wave at the front and some darling little curls on the nape of her neck—definitely natural— whereas Miss Jackson's hair was permed. Everyone had noticed this after the Christmas holidays. Miss Chalmers was slim and graceful whereas Miss Jackson was inclined towards plumpness and wore glasses. With the first goal for the Earlswood District Eleven, Miss Chalmers and Miss Jackson changed places with each other in Jane's heart.

The triple clash of hockey sticks marked the resumption of play still watched intently, though not very intelligently, by the grey eyes on the other side of the fence. Jane did not have the slightest idea what 'offside' meant or what the referee wanted when she stretched her arm out to one side. She had never volunteered for stick practice, though eligible as a secondary school pupil. Occasionally, when out walking with her father, she had heard him pooh-poohing the game and comparing the players unfavourably with their male counterparts in football. Privately, she had resolved never to demean herself by becoming one of their number. But now—

could her father possibly have been wrong? Surely, if he were to witness Miss Chalmers' performance he would change his mind.

Suddenly, Jane felt a drop of rain on her hand followed by another, then another. Play continued for a while but when the shower developed into a downpour the whistle blew and the players hurried from the field. Jane, still on her bicycle, remained propped against the fence, trembling with self-consciousness. The two elevens emerged from the field only a few yards off and Miss Chalmers approached smiling. "You'd better come and shelter with us," she invited.

"We can't neglect our only supporter," said another voice. It was Miss McTurk, the science teacher, who also played for the Earlswood District Eleven.

Excited and triumphant, Jane dismounted and wheeled her bike into the school grounds.

The two elevens were now hurrying into the Annexe which housed the school dining room and kitchens. Two long tables were already set with cups, saucers and plates. The other tables in the dining room were scrubbed and bare, the chairs having been stacked upside down on top. The little blackboard on the wall at the door still bore Friday's menu—lentil soup, mince, stewed steak, fried haddock, steamed pudding, pears and custard. Jane smiled to herself. How could she have anticipated an adventure like this when she had last sat here!

Jane had school dinners every day along with Madge and Fiona. If they hurried across the playground from their last class, they usually managed to get seats at the end of tables one, two or three which were nearest to the table used by the staff. Miss Jackson lunched there twice a week, quite unconscious of the scrutiny of her three admirers who would speculate on her every mouthful, for the teachers, who paid more, had a different menu. Even when she did not come for lunch, the teachers' table was still a matter of absorbing interest. Every move was invested with more than ordinary significance. If Miss Craig entered in company with Miss Brown on Monday and Tuesday but with Miss Stewart on Wednesday, the girls were sure that there had been a quarrel. Similarly, if Miss Thomson left by herself after a hasty lunch. The silver-haired Miss Hood and the salt-and-pepper Miss Irving were inseparables. As both were attractive in spite of advancing years, legend had it that they had been engaged to two brothers, following whose death in a prison camp they had vowed eternal mutual fidelity.

The hockey players dispersed to the gymnasium on the upper floor for a shower and a change of clothing but Miss Chalmers, beckoning to Jane, went into the kitchen. She pointed to two polythene boxes and a pile of large plates.

"I know you're wet on the outside, Jane," she said, "but you're probably dryer underneath than we are. Will you put out these sandwiches—tomato from this box, gammon from the other?"

A flood of joy engulfed Jane. Miss Chalmers had asked her to do something to help. If she had been asked to scrub the floor, she would have dropped to her knees with a hymn in her heart. Like St. Columba she would have been happy to

'Keep even the smallest door,
The furthest door, the darkest, coldest door,
The door that is least used, the stiffest door'

if in so doing, she could please Miss Chalmers. She spread out the plates and with consummate care made a little pyramid of sandwiches on each.

Miss Chalmers returned.

"That's splendid, Jane," she said. "Now will you take them through to the tables and come back for the biscuits."

With her tongue extended as though to help her balance, Jane carried the plates through to the dining room and placed them reverently on the tables. She built the biscuits up in similar fashion.

Through the high bare windows, the rain fell steadily and Jane prayed that it would continue for a long time.

The hockey players, dry and changed, entered and took their seats. Jane looked at them curiously. It was no longer possible, now that they had changed, to distinguish the Earlswood District Eleven from their guests, and the brightly stockinged figures now looked drab and ordinary, though two or three looked young enough to be Sixth-year girls. Those who had seemed youthfully sturdy and active on the hockey pitch, a sort of Super Senior Girl, suddenly emerged as rather blousy, bourgeois housewives, or so it seemed to Jane.

Miss McTurk poured out the tea and signed to Jane to take a seat at the end of the row next to herself and Miss Chalmers.

The talk became general.

"My goodness, I needed that cup."

"Me too. What lovely sandwiches."

"Have another one then."

"Thanks. Just look at that rain."

Miss Chalmers turned to Jane.

"Are you in the Junior Eleven?" she asked.

Jane swallowed. She decided not to mention her previous scorn of the game. As for inclusion in the Junior Eleven, she was on safer ground for it was not open to First-year pupils. She sought to explain but the word 'eligible' eluded her. 'Legible' and 'legitimate' had trembled in confusion on her lips. The first she knew to be wrong, the second she was uncertain about but it sounded good and after a moment's hesitation she had replied.

"No, I'm not legitimate."

Miss Chalmers eyebrows had arched quizzically but she smiled in a kindly fashion, she seemed to understand.

"Well, never mind, Jane," she said. "Perhaps you will be next year. Have you got sisters in the school?"

Jane felt herself reddening. How she hated this kind of question. All her life she had had to confess to being one of that particularly despised social group—an only child. The usual rejoinder from the inquirer (who was invariably at the centre of a clutch of siblings) was a jeering assurance that she must certainly be spoiled. Jane, aware that she had been given most of what she wanted by an indulgent father, had had nothing to reply.

But Miss Chalmers did not seem to think it odd and only asked, "Who all lives at home then?"

Jane reddened still further. This was another question she usually hated.

"Just my father and myself," she stammered. Suddenly, she felt very near tears.

Again, the kindly smile and Miss Chalmers' eyes softened. She put an arm round Jane's shoulders and gave her an affectionate squeeze.

"I expect you mean a lot to your father," she said.

There was a reassuring echo from Miss McTurk and the biscuits went round again.

Jane gulped.

"I've already had two," she said bashfully.

"Well, have another," said the jolly Miss McTurk. "This is your afternoon tea, you know."

***

Legitimate! That was not the word she had been groping after. What did it mean anyway? She consulted the dictionary. It said: 'lawful: lawfully begotten: genuine: fairly deduced: following by natural sequence: authorised by usage.' It was the second definition which attracted her attention. So legitimate was one of *those* words, those mysterious words on which she had stumbled so frequently in recent months; words which brought her within reach of the veil which still hung between herself and the adult world, a veil which she dared not lift; words which brought a wordless awareness of a whole range of human experience beyond her understanding.

It had started a few months previously when she had been reading about Mary Queen of Scots who was said to have a brother who was a bastard.

"Daddy, what's a bastard?" she had asked.

Mr. Purdie had looked up from his newspaper and cleared his throat, very much aware of the solemn eyes fixed on him.

"Well," he began hesitantly, "that's something that Mummy could have explained to you better than I can."

His expression softened.

"You'll understand when you're older, Jane," he said very gently.

And he lifted his newspaper up, effectively shutting himself off from her eyes.

With the dictionary now in her hand, it occurred to her that she could quite easily turn to letter b. The veil swayed provocatively in the face of her curiosity but she closed the book with a bang. Anyway, she still did not know what legitimate really meant. It had been the same with adultery—'violation of the marriage bed' the dictionary said, but that had not really been at all helpful.

You couldn't even escape from it in the Bible. Words which had seemed as clear as daylight, suddenly became invested with hidden meaning—Old Testament Joseph had been invited by Potiphar's wife to *lie* with her. David, King of Israel *lay* with Bathsheba, wife of Uriah the Hittite.

Well. It didn't really matter. She had had a heavenly afternoon and the day after tomorrow was Monday which started with two periods of English with Miss Chalmers.

She concluded her account of the afternoon's adventures with a few poetic lines in which she recognised with satisfaction something of an echo of Sir Walter Scott's address to Caledonia. (The class was doing "The Lay of the Last Minstrel" with Miss Chalmers that term.)

"Oh gracious lady, fair and sweet,
I lay my heart down at your feet.
Lady so beautiful and dear,
Your lilting voice, I love to hear.
Lady adored, oh, May I be
Forever pleasing unto thee.
Lady supreme, what power on earth
Could tear me from thy sterling worth
Which makes my heart's love blossom forth!"

Well pleased, she unrolled the paper from her machine and put it into a large envelope marked Private Papers.

Mr. Purdie was dozing by the fire.

"I'm going to bed, Daddy," she whispered but he did not waken.

All she wanted now was to be cosy underneath the bed-clothes so that, undisturbed, she could relive and again and again relive the events of the afternoon.

As she drifted off to sleep, she came to just sufficiently to murmur, "I know—it was 'eligible'."

Chapter II
Mr. Purdie's Life History

George Purdie continued to doze in the easy-chair by the fire, for the room was overheated in spite of the dying embers. The chintz-covers of the living room suite sported a gay pattern but were much in need of a clean; here and there the soft pile of the recently purchased carpet showed a stain, and an untidy assortment of personal possessions was scattered throughout the room.

The fruit-bowl on the sideboard was filled with elastic bands, drawing-pins and pencil stubs; while round it, in disarray, stood half-a-dozen apples, two oranges and three bananas. Also on the sideboard lay a handful of coins, Jane's knitting and two exercise books, a packet of biscuits, a train timetable and the washing-up mop, laid down in a moment of abstraction. The mantelpiece bore witness to the same lack of care. Between the candlesticks at either end and the china cat in the middle were a match-box, some paper clips and a booklet of daily Bible readings. The Radio Times lay on the floor beside George's shoes which were standing at a rakish angle to each other. The typewriter still graced the table, together with boxes of typing and carbon paper, rubber, biro and a packet of mints. From the bookcase in the corner peered some handsomely bound volumes of Dickens, Scott, Thackeray and the works of the poets, interspersed with schoolgirl stories and children's classics. The curtains were frayed at the inner edges and every item of furniture was covered in a film of dust.

No matter. It was Saturday evening, the only night in the week when George Purdie was able to relax fully.

There had been a succession of daily helps over the five preceding years but for the moment, George was without. They had all presented initially as capable and trustworthy women, each anxious in her own way to make the home comfortable for Mr. Purdie and Jane, but after varying periods of time withdrew. They had all had their faults and corresponding virtues but the want of housewifely supervision during working hours had led in each case to an inevitable decline in standards.

Sadie, Mr Purdie learned from a neighbour, never turned up before eleven thirty a.m. but willingly worked on into the evening, which meant that Mr. Purdie felt obliged to drive her home, an offer which she never refused.

Cissy, on the other hand, was an early bird and usually arrived along with the paper-boy before eight o'clock, while father and daughter were still at breakfast. Following one bitterly cold morning when she arrived sniffing and shivering, it had become her practice to join them at the table for what was supposed to be a quick cup of tea, but Mr. Purdie had an irritating suspicion that she was in no hurry to start her work when, twenty minutes later, they left her comfortably installed behind the teapot with cigarettes, lighter and ashtray spread out before her.

Bridie came and went unseen but eventually forsook them to become a lollipop woman when a change in her husband's shifts made it necessary to fit in more closely with her children's school hours. It had been some time before a replacement was found, during which period the degree of chaos grew to such an extent that the elderly Mrs. Reid lasted one day only, having found it impossible to dig her way through the accumulated disorder. This had really spurred Mr. Purdie into action and before Mary arrived he spent an entire weekend tidying, dusting and cleaning in case she too would take flight. Mary had worked well but had an alcoholic husband and she eventually took a heart attack, worn out with anxiety and overwork.

It seemed likely, however, that they would soon have someone else, as a neighbour's daily had been able to recommend a friend. It was a relief to know that once again there would be some degree of control over the ever-advancing tide of domestic disorder, but George sighed deeply when he thought of the effort he would have to make before the advent of Mrs. McSporran in order to prevent instant flight.

George Purdie was a conscientious man who had experienced household anxieties from an early age. As the eldest of six, he had always been expected to help at home—to run errands, to tramp the blankets in the bath at spring-cleaning time, to mind the baby when his mother had been busy with one or other of his brothers and sisters. When, at the age of twelve, his father died, he found himself very much his mother's support, both financially and as a confidante. He had risen at five a.m. in order to deliver milk and had got a frequent 'palmy' from the headmaster for lateness. He still remembered, with some resentment, how badly his hand smarted from the belt on cold days.

Then, he had delivered evening papers after school and spent the whole of every Saturday morning on a depressing round collecting payments from his milk customers, with only an occasional tip to relieve the monotony. There was constant anxiety at home over the payment of gas, electricity and rent, and George had early accustomed himself to switching off unnecessary lights and to taking his mother's place at the counter of the local grocery shop when, on the day preceding the pay-out of widows' pensions, it was usually necessary to ask for goods on credit.

An intelligent boy, he had wished to pursue his education perhaps to University level but was driven at fourteen by economic pressures and a harassed mother into the treadmill of employment where a weekly wage superseded the need of an active mind for education and training. After a series of dead-end jobs, George eventually found himself a bookkeeper in a firm of building contractors where he had risen to the position of chief wages clerk, a job in which he saw security and a reasonable income.

Marriage had brought its share of sweetness and suffering. In his future wife's family background, the struggling young clerk saw all that had been missing from his own life. Elspeth's father was a minister and life at the manse with its book-shelves and its spaciousness, its formal atmosphere and comparative affluence, approximated to his ideal of gracious living. Elspeth herself, the only unmarried daughter still at home, was a teacher, having followed the lead of her mother and one of her sisters. As her father's daughter, she could do no other than organise the Brownies, help at Bazaars, teach in the Sunday School and offer her services to family, neighbours and congregation when required, which was frequent, especially after the marriage of her sisters. She had known all the strictness of a Calvinistic household with none of the humour or tenderness which her gentle nature had needed and at twenty-five she found herself a useful, though not particularly happy member of society, functioning rather automatically within church and school and conscious that her own life had never properly begun.

George Purdie was her first and only admirer. His old-fashioned chivalrous ideas had awakened her dormant femininity and she had learned to detach herself from her family sufficiently to be able to laugh at what George regarded as its middle-class splendour. George had been received courteously, if rather stiffly, by her parents and sisters, but for Elspeth his courtship had opened the door of a cage from which the imprisoned bird was determined to escape. Escape she did after a protracted engagement, during which George struggled manfully to find a surer foothold on the economic ladder, for he was resolved that his Elspeth should experience no diminution of home comforts through marriage to himself.

Lingering memories of his father-in-law's home still activated him, though not always consciously. Occasionally, he recalled with a quiet smile a conversational attempt by Mr. Carmichael when he had called for Elspeth after a football match. With the book which he had been reading balanced casually on the arm of his chair, Mr. Carmichael had listened benevolently to George's account of the match and had varied his parenthetical comments with the odd question.

"What exactly *is* a corner, Mr. Purdie?" he had demanded.

George knew that his explanation had gone in one ear and out the other.

Within a year of marriage their first child, Jane, was born and for Elspeth the experience of motherhood had brought a sense of deep fulfilment. George shared her joy. His own parental instinct was strong and he wanted nothing more than to maintain the home life which he and

Elspeth had created together. Eighteen months later, Elspeth was again pregnant but miscarried after a difficult pregnancy. Their mutual grief was deep. George felt that they should not risk another pregnancy but Elspeth longed for a second child. Again, she became pregnant and again miscarried. This time George was determined to be master of the situation and for a time Elspeth was content to accept his decision, mainly because of poor general health. Jane was now five. Elspeth was thirty, in outward respects vastly different from the retiring daughter of the manse of ten years back. At a deeper level, however, her chilly Calvinistic upbringing had left an ineradicable mark; the woman in her had been sacrificed for a principle and the woman still craved expression. George found himself engulfed and against medical advice there was a fourth, then a fifth pregnancy, each necessitating long spells in hospital. Both ended in miscarriage and the fifth cost Elspeth her life.

In his early forties, therefore, George found himself a widower with an eight-year-old daughter to care for. Elspeth's parents were both dead and his own mother, crippled with arthritis, had made her home with her youngest daughter in England. Two brothers had emigrated with their wives and children and he had little contact since his marriage with the brother and sister who still resided in Glasgow. Marriage for George had set the final seal on his aversion to the hand-to-mouth way of life in which he had been brought up, and contact with his immediate family circle had been only tenuously maintained. Jane had five cousins but barely knew them.

Elspeth likewise had lost touch with her sisters though neither had moved far out of Glasgow. Close relationships had never existed in the manse. George's acceptance within the family circle had been on a superficial basis and though he had acquired some prestige in the eyes of Elspeth's parents through becoming the father of their only grandchild, the link was severed with their death. Isabel and Grace had no great interest in either their brother-in-law or their small niece, and their formal offers of help had been rejected by George.

Nor had there been any invigorating support from friends for George and Elspeth had pursued an isolated domestic course; Elspeth, because in home, husband and child, she had achieved all that she had missed in her busy lonely twenties; George, because he was content if Elspeth was content.

With Elspeth's death, George bowed his head, as he had bowed his head all the way along the line to the somewhat limited way of life which she had established in their home. He mourned her loss and saw in it the need to merge in himself the maternal and paternal functions hitherto divided between them. During the first two terrible days, Jane had never stopped crying. Then, with the resilience of childhood, she stepped out into a new world, hand-in-hand with a father-mother in whom she invested not only all that the father already possessed of her heart but all that had been held in reserve for the mother who had so frequently been too unwell to accept it.

Though in no way lacking in manliness, George became something of a mother-bird towards his one fledgling, doubly precious because of the four little brothers and sisters who had never properly existed. From the moment when he had coaxed the weeping child out from beneath the parental bed where she had sought refuge in her first access of grief, he had devoted himself to her utterly. He had bought her the much-coveted bicycle, though his own heart had been heavy, the day after the funeral. Then followed many patient hours on the quiet road at the side of the house while Jane wobbled breathlessly on the shining new two-wheeler, her loss quickly put aside; now nestling against the stalwart figure who held her steady, now reproving him for holding her too closely.

He it was who bandaged the skinned knees and mended the broken doll; who dried her eyes when her sums would not come out right and who rejoiced with her when she had full marks for her spelling; who took her for picnics in the summer and shared with her the cosy, fireside evenings of winter. She was his little woman and he adored her with all the love of his faithful heart.

Jane, for her part, alternately loved and scolded him; clung to him and dispensed with him; beckoned him and dismissed him with all the imperiousness of childhood.

George's housekeeping was rough and ready but there was nothing he would not tackle. In an attempt to cut down on dish-washing, he made the soup-plates do duty for the second course; the milk-bottle for the jug; and, as like as not, the loaf stood on the table in its wrapper. It usually took an accident, like an overturned sauce bottle, to remind him that the tablecloth required changing. Jane was oblivious to the many crudities of the ménage and enjoyed nothing quite so much as Saturday tea when, with their fingers, they slurped fish and chips, pie and chips, chicken and chips or haggis and chips, usually deluged with tomato-sauce, from the newspaper-wrapped trays supplied by the local fish and chip shop.

He had, of course, considered the possibility of remarriage without really desiring it. Twelve months elapsed before he had managed to detach emotionally from Elspeth and by this time he was so entrenched in his new domestic routine that he rarely gave the matter more than a fleeting thought. At business, the pace was brisk; at home, his horizon was bounded by his responsibility towards Jane. As he relaxed in his fireside chair on a Saturday evening, Mr. Purdie told himself many a time that he was a lucky man.

Chapter III
The Classroom

The last echoes of the school bell had died away. The last of the shuffling feet had vanished behind the closed doors of the classrooms and the last chattering voice was silent. It had at one time been intended that classes should march along the corridors in neat lines behind their class captain, the vice-captain bringing up the rear, but this was an ideal rarely achieved in practice. The primary classes had certainly been more amenable to discipline of this kind. Indeed, Miss McKirdy, teacher of Primary 5, whose brother was a soldier, was very keen on lane discipline and had exhorted successive decades of ten-year-olds to march two by two, heads up, lips tightly sealed, as they moved from their own classroom to the Art or Needlework Rooms and back again.

"Primary 5 is famed throughout the school for its marching," she would say brightly. "You must keep the tradition alive."

The older girls had all been processed by Miss McKirdy during their passage through Primary 5, but having reached the magnificent heights of secondary school status, the tight-lipped marching was discarded by way of emancipation and Miss Armstrong, the headmistress, had decided not to enforce it.

The result was a rather casual shuffle between one class and the next with a hastily exchanged inquest on the lesson concluded or an eleventh-hour peep at the textbook en route for the next lesson. Miss Caskie, the Principal Maths teacher, who kept habitual vigil at the top of the upper stairway, would survey with disfavour the amorphous mass of classes clattering and shuffling up to the top corridor.

"Keep to the right there," was her rallying cry, to which from time immemorial the girls had made automatic response.

Girls from the top corridor classrooms slithered down the east stairway; girls from the lower floor struggled up the west stairway. West moved east and east moved west. Gowned staff followed in their wake. Of a sudden peace descended and the next lesson began.

Miss Chalmers had been delayed by Miss Armstrong while Secondary IA assembled in her classroom. The girls had been asked to do a home exercise in ink consisting of the General Analysis of a sentence and the parsing of certain words in it. In preparation for her arrival, exercise books were brought out.

With quiet pleasure Jane surveyed the neat page in front of her, planned in accordance with Miss Chalmers' instructions—the sentence at the top with the clauses and their description set out in tabular form. Lastly, the parsing. For Jane, it had been a labour of love and she looked forward confidently to a good mark.

The minutes ticked past. No sign of Miss Chalmers. The near silence gave way to growing chatter.

"I thought it was a silly sentence," said Dorothy with a yawn. Dorothy hated anything that required effort.

"What's silly about it?" asked Madge, Jane's friend.

"Och, all these silly clauses," replied Dorothy scowling at her exercise book. She read the sentence aloud. "'The neighbour, into whose care the mother had entrusted her baby, started up when she heard the approaching footsteps.' Why didn't she look after the baby herself?"

"Well, it's only a sentence," put in Jane. "It's not supposed to mean anything. It's just for us to analyse."

But Dorothy was not to be put off.

"My mother looked after all of us without any neighbours," she said with sudden incisiveness, "three of us. She keeps us all clean and tidy. A clean blouse and underwear every day, no holes in our socks and our buttons sewed on as soon as they come off."

She pushed back a curling tendril of hair and stared hard at Jane, who suddenly became conscious of a button missing from her cardigan.

"She says she has put us all to a good school and she wants to make sure that we don't let the school down," Dorothy continued with a superior air.

"If you worked harder, you would get better marks and you wouldn't let yourself down," chipped in Fiona.

Dorothy glared at her.

"I'd rather have low marks and neat clothes than be like some people," she snapped maliciously. "What's the point of being the teacher's pet if you can't keep yourself tidy?"

Jane knew that the remark was directed at her. She loved her schoolwork and her steady application had frequently been commended. She would have liked to reply but could not. This was the kind of below-the-belt blow which froze her into silence. The other girls, sensitive on her behalf, said nothing. Dorothy was aware that she had overstepped the mark but was unable to draw back.

"My mother says your mother would still be alive if she hadn't gone on having babies," she went on. "She says your father should have had more sense."

Jane suddenly found her voice.

"It was nothing to do with him," she faltered. "My mother just wanted me to have sisters and brothers, that's all."

Dorothy laughed mockingly.

"Nothing to do with him!" she echoed. "So that's all you know."

Janette and Elaine, her cronies, tittered.

Jane said nothing. Her face became expressionless. Unconscious defences claimed her and woodenly she faced round to the front again, inadvertently overturning her ink-bottle which streamed down the open page of her exercise book and over her grey skirt. The girls sitting nearest gasped in horror. Madge drew some blotting-paper from her desk and offered it but Jane did not move.

At this moment Miss Chalmers entered the room. The girls rose as was their custom and returned her greeting. Mechanically, Jane followed suit and as she occupied a front seat, her skirt was exposed. The stained exercise book was unpleasantly conspicuous.

Miss Chalmers noticed it immediately.

"What's this?" she demanded.

Jane's eyes were lowered. She could not trust herself to speak and felt her colour rising.

"She knocked over her ink-bottle, Miss Chalmers," volunteered Madge, "but it was an accident."

"I'm sure it was," replied Miss Chalmers, "but you know, Jane, you're not allowed to have an ink-bottle on the desk. That's why we have inkwells."

It should have been so simple to explain that the inkwell was dirty and she did not want to clog her pen. But her attention was riveted on the ink-sodden page. Her mind juggled with impossible solutions as the clock on the wall ticked loudly in the suddenly silent room. She was dumb and it was as though a hundred thousand tongues were struggling to find utterance, to tell with what loving care every letter of every word had been formed, because the eye that would see it was the eye of someone who mattered, and the mind would linger momentarily on Jane while the hand assigned a mark.

Miss Chalmers took a thickly folded blotting-paper from her desk and pressed it down on Jane's exercise book. Then, she turned her attention to Jane's skirt.

"You had better blot up what you can, Jane," she said kindly, "and then go to Miss MacBride in the laundry. I'll give you a note."

Mechanically, Jane stumbled to her feet. Once more, words clamoured for expression but the lips were silent. Today, Wednesday, was a highlight in Jane's week because it was one of the two days when IA had a double period of English, twice forty minutes, with Miss Chalmers. What did the skirt matter? And it hurt that Miss Chalmers was dismissing her, however concerned she might be about the stain. How could she possibly know how precious these eighty minutes were! Anyway, she could not have been happy in Miss Chalmers' presence with an ink-stained skirt. And wouldn't Dorothy Reid crow!

She moved towards the door and suddenly found her voice.

"Yes, Miss Chalmers," she muttered miserably.

***

Stout Miss MacBride had been kind and helpful after her first exclamation of horror at the sight of the ink-stained Jane. The skirt was steeped, washed and hung up on the pulley while Jane was despatched back to her classroom wearing her coat.

The lesson had only run halfway on her return but for Jane the glory of the day had departed and she resumed her seat dully.

One by one the girls were reciting a passage of twenty lines or so from "The Lay of the Last Minstrel" which they had been required to memorise.

"Breathes there the man, with soul so dead,
Who never to himself hath said
This is my own, my native land!" chanted Angela Brown in her sing-song voice. In Primary 2 Angela had been acknowledged the best reader in the class. The mannerisms which had been appealing in a seven-year-old, however, now tended to raise a quiet smile in teacher and pupils alike, from the unconsciously arched eyebrows which gave her a rather surprised expression to the exaggerated articulation and the head which nodded ceaseless emphasis.

"Whose heart hath ne'er within him burn'd,
As home his footsteps he hath turn'd,
From wandering on a foreign strand!" quavered the mouselike Monica with the usual terror-stricken expression which no one took seriously, since it alternated too rapidly with an impish grin.

"If such there breathe, go, mark him well;
For him no minstrel raptures swell;
High though his titles, proud his name,
Boundless his wealth as wish can claim;" came the toneless rendering of Jean Dunne. Jean was gifted with a

retentive memory and was never known to miss a word, but the flatness of her voice and the intensity of her sibilants sapped the beauty from whatever passage she recited. The letter 's' always seemed to recur twice as often when Jean was reciting and imparted something sinister to her performance, as though a top secret was being relayed.

"Despite those titles, power and pelf,
The wretch, concentred all in self,
Living, shall forfeit fair renown,
And, doubly dying, shall go down
To the vile dust, from whence he sprung,
Unwept, unhonour'd and unsung."

Dorothy's rather pompous rendering of the immortal lines made officious proclamation that she had elocution lessons.

"O Caledonia! Stern and wild,
Meet nurse for a poetic child!"

Fiona also was an elocutionist but had absorbed the art of enunciation effortlessly.

"Land of brown heath and shaggy wood,
Land of the mountain and the flood,
Land of my sires! what mortal hand
Can e'er untie the filial band,
That knits me to thy rugged strand!" recited Madge in her matter of fact voice which successfully cloaked a sensitive appreciation of the meaning of the passage.

The spring sunshine streamed in through the windows and fell across Miss Chalmers as she presided in a pleasantly relaxed fashion at her desk. Roused eventually from her misery, Jane looked up and allowed herself the luxury of gazing on the adored one.

By any standards Miss Chalmers was an attractive woman but to the lovelorn Jane she was the embodiment of all that was lovely. She had a crop of curly brown hair which she kept short and well-shaped. She was slender and moved with easy grace.

Passive contemplation no longer satisfied Jane. She longed to make a response and her reviving spirits fell to zero when the ink-stained exercise book obtruded itself again on her attention. The presentation of the exercise would have provided her with just such an outlet, but of this she had been deprived, and despair once more claimed her.

Usually, she enjoyed being called upon to recite but Dorothy's remarks about her father and the unborn babies, followed by the accident, had had a disintegrating effect. Dorothy then had solved the mystery, had crossed the line, had eaten the forbidden fruit. Thus, Jane divided those who knew from those who did not. A series of metaphors cloaking dimly apprehended facts flitted across her mind and deepened her unhappiness.

Miss Chalmers' voice interrupted her meditations.

"Jane, I think you're the only one who hasn't had a turn. Would you like to try?"

Jane had applied herself so thoroughly to the memorising of this passage that she could have recited it backwards if need be. How she had longed to recite aloud to Miss Chalmers the very lines which she had paraphrased in her heroine's honour. But the first line escaped her. She stood in her place, painfully conscious that she was wearing her coat. Her retentive faculty was shorn of its tentacles and the words were washed away into a sea of tears.

"I can't do it," she whispered, overwhelmed by silent sobbing.

"Let's leave it for today then, Jane," said Miss Chalmers kindly.

Quickly redirecting the attention of the class, she brought the lesson to a close.

"Now girls, there are only a few minutes till the end of the period. Will you read over the next two chapters of your home reader before next Wednesday?"

The clamour of the bell broke in on the lesson and Miss Chalmers gave a sign for the class to dismiss.

As Jane filed past with the others, Miss Chalmers gave her hand a reassuring squeeze.

"My heart used to go pit-a-pat when I had to recite in class," she said understandingly.

Jane stood still, her eyes on the floor, overwhelmingly conscious of Miss Chalmers' nearness. Her eyes travelled from her own lace-ups to Miss Chalmers' neatly-fitting court shoes with the little bow in front. Her glance lingered there momentarily. Then, because Miss Chalmers did not hasten away, she was impelled to look up into the face that smiled down on her. Worship filled her soul.

To Miss Chalmers' other qualities, could she have found the words, she would have added the tenderness of a Madonna.

***

"I really do love her," said Jane earnestly to Madge and Fiona, as they made their way to the station after school. "I simply can't describe how much I love her. It was awful when the ink-bottle spilled but, d'you know, it was worth it to get that lovely smile from her at the end."

Jane did not quite mean this. The memory of the ink-splashed exercise book was not so readily effaced but the warm hand squeeze and the accompanying smile had not been without its compensating effect.

Though not smitten, as Jane was, by Miss Chalmers' charms, Madge was sufficiently under the spell of Miss Jackson to understand her feelings.

"It was the most wonderful moment in my life," went on Jane. "It really was."

"You said that after the hockey match," retorted Fiona, who had allowed herself to be carried along on the emotional wave in which the two others, in varying degrees, had become engulfed, but whose affections had tended to remain at a more sober level.

Jane groped for an explanation, as much for her own benefit as for Fiona's.

"But this was different, Fiona," she protested. "She was just being friendly at the hockey match. But today she seemed to know how awful I was feeling and wanted to help."

She stopped in her tracks.

"She was just like an angel reaching down from heaven," she said soulfully.

Madge surveyed her with interest.

"Y–yes," she agreed slowly. "But I still like Miss Jackson best. And it's not so long since Miss Jackson was your favourite teacher too."

"I know," replied Jane simply. "I loved Miss Jackson for eleven weeks and three days. But I'll love Miss Chalmers forever and ever."

"No, you won't," retorted the practical Fiona. "You'll stop loving her when someone starts loving you."

Jane stared.

"I could never be half as wonderful or beautiful as Miss Chalmers," she answered honestly.

"You don't know," replied Fiona with a knowing smile which neither Jane nor Madge had seen before. "Someone thinks *I'm* beautiful," she said with meaning.

Such an astounding remark as this brought both her listeners to a standstill and Fiona underwent a close scrutiny. She was a neatly made, pretty thirteen-year-old with fair curly hair and a ready smile. In imagination, her friends placed her in the scales alongside their respective idols and found her sadly wanting. But their curiosity was nevertheless roused.

"How do you know someone thinks you're beautiful?" demanded Madge.

"Ah!" The monosyllable was deliberately protracted and Fiona's eyes sparkled mischievously.

"Is it someone in the class?" asked Madge wonderingly.

"In the class!" echoed Fiona with contempt. "Of course not!"

The school they attended was for girls only.

An appalling thought struck Jane.

"It's—it's not Miss Chalmers, is it?" she asked in a stricken tone.

Fiona laughed delightedly and shook her head.

Jane breathed a sigh of relief. She did not much mind who the mysterious admirer might be so long as she did not have to compete with Fiona for Miss Chalmers' affections.

"He stares at me all the time in the Bible Class," Fiona conceded at length, "and last Sunday he walked home with me afterwards."

The announcement was made with triumph but it fell on disappointed ears.

"A boy!" exclaimed Jane. "But boys are aggressive!"

Madge also felt out of her depth but expressed herself rather less forcibly.

"Do you not think you're too young for boys, Fiona?" she queried, unconsciously echoing her mother who was at present concerned about Madge's fifteen-year-old sister, Betty.

They had reached the railway bridge at this point and a trundling noise from the tunnel beneath heralded the approach of the train, so with the question left unanswered they took to their heels. Madge's hat flew off as they descended the stairs precipitately, and Jane's case burst open disgorging books and jotters all the way down, but having retrieved their possessions, they came up panting alongside the train.

Cheeks flushed by the chase, they sank back in their seats and Madge surveyed the muddy crown of her hat.

"That's the third time it's blown off this month," she said ruefully. "Mum said last time if it happened again, she would put an elastic on it."

"Donald and Sandy are always needing their caps cleaned," said Fiona, referring to her two younger brothers. "There's a cap-snatching campaign on at the Academy."

"Just look at this," sighed Jane holding up a mud-spleutered jotter. "*And* my French grammar—*and* my Palgrave's Golden Treasury. Thank goodness it was only the covers that got wet."

She rubbed the brown paper covers down with the sleeve of her coat and rearranged the contents of her case.

"Maybe Mum'll not notice my hat this time," said Madge. "She's busy making new spring dresses for Betty and me. We got the material on Saturday. Mine is turquoise and Betty's is green. She's done the cutting out and she's getting on with Betty's first because she has a party to go to."

"Whose party is it?" asked Jane.

"It's Joyce Monro's," replied Madge. "She and her twin brother are sixteen on the 20th. Betty says they always give great parties. There's such a big family of them."

"Donald will be eleven next week," observed Fiona without enthusiasm. "Some of his friends are coming to tea. Hope to goodness they're not as noisy as Sandy's were last time. Mum organised a treasure hunt for them and they nearly wrecked the house."

"Is he having a birthday cake?" asked Madge.

"Oh, I suppose so," replied Fiona. "Mum usually makes us a birthday cake each. Last year, she decorated Donald's with blue and white icing to match the school colours."

Jane was silent. It was with a pang that she listened to the narration of family happenings such as these homemade birthday cakes, the threat of hat elastic to be sewn on, the transformation of cloth, buttons, zips and thread into clothes while a pregnant sewing machine purred loving accompaniment; a house made noisy with the sound of scrambling feet and boyish voices; the casual naming of brothers and sisters by those who had them, apparently unconscious of the vastness of their wealth; the ordinary events of other people's experiences resounded in Jane's ears like the echoes of a jubilee she had never known.

"Robert was five last month," she announced defensively. "He'll be starting school next term. I've knitted him a pullover."

Robert was Jane's pretend-brother and was the youngest of that wraith-like coterie of babies who had somehow failed to complete the journey from the other world into this. In her imagination, Jane had aligned them with Sir Joshua Reynolds' 'Cherub Choir' which was one of the pictures in her illustrated Bible. This was her most vivid impression of them, proclaiming as it did not only their prime existence elsewhere but also their individuality, which was something in which Jane believed most firmly. The cherub at the front Jane had at an early date identified with herself. She, alone of the five, had emerged from the womb of timelessness, and the outward-gazing little face, therefore, appeared to have an awareness of the earth-world to come which was denied the other four.

Jane was fully aware of the dates when the little lives had been prematurely curtailed. She had given them all names and birthdays, and though the faces were blurred, she could describe in some detail the personalities of each. James and Robert, named after two of her father's brothers, had celebrated their eleventh and fifth birthdays on Bonfire Night and St. Valentine's Day respectively; and Isobel and Grace, called after her mother's sisters, would be eight and seven on Halloweens and Hogmanay. James took after Mr. Purdie and was her favourite brother. Isobel had been delicate since infancy and had never been able to participate in her big sister's activities. Grace was a smaller roly-poly version of herself and Robert was the tough guy of the family, seldom seen without his pistols and holster.

Madge and Fiona knew all about Jane's pretend family. Jane was touched by their interest, they who had experience of the real thing. Madge and Fiona were the only two people who knew about them and she chatted to them easily about James and his examination successes or Isobel and her asthma, entirely innocent of deceptive intention, secure in the semi-conscious awareness that these friends understood the distinction between truth and fact.

The train slowed to a halt at Bridgebank and the three girls dismounted to part company outside the station. Jane turned right while the other two turned left. There was an exchange of cheerios.

"Hope Isobel's asthma's better," shouted Madge.

Jane waved and trudged up the hill.

Chapter IV
Mr. Purdie Meets Miss Chalmers

The Purdies occupied a roomy bungalow with back and front garden on the outskirts of Glasgow. Winter had brought Mr. Purdie release from his gardening labours but with the advent of spring the annual growth had again commenced. The hedge, which grew higher than the wall at the front and the railings at the back, was ready for its first trim, and weeds were already beginning to push their intrusive way up through the red chips on either side of the paving stones, and through the dark brown sods on the flower beds.

An early spring twilight was descending when Jane arrived home. For a moment, she was startled by the light in the hall and the sound of the washing machine from the kitchen. Then she remembered that Mrs. McSporran, the new cleaner, was to be there that afternoon. Her heart sank. With her leave-taking of Madge and Fiona, the misery occasioned by the overturned ink-bottle had reclaimed her, and she did not feel capable of mustering the effort to meet a new personality.

With deliberate slowness, she fumbled for her key. She shrank from the idea of being welcomed to her home by an utter stranger and was tempted to shut the door softly and creep into her own bedroom unseen, there to shed a few miserable tears. The creak of the hinge, however, which Mr. Purdie was always going to oil but never did, broke the silence which followed the completion of a tubful's wash and Mrs. McSporran appeared at the kitchen door.

Jane's first impression was that of largeness, for the new daily filled the doorway. Mrs. McSporran had been something of a belle in her day but over the years she had sacrificed her once lissom figure to eight children and advancing age. She was toothless from choice, having found the sustained effort of adjusting to dentures too much for her. Her crowning glory, however, was her hair, a glossy chestnut in which there was more than the hint of a tint, and which she contrived daily to twist into a beehive style wonderful to behold and adding several inches to her height. Her heart was of the kindest but her appearance was not encouraging. At fifty-six, with twenty-two grandchildren to her credit, she eschewed restraining garments, feeling more relaxed in a loose-fitting jumper and a pair of amply swirling flairs, the zip of which had to bear the continued strain of her plumpness. Early memories of a picture-book illustration of the giant's wife confronting Jack as he emerged from the copper swam hazily before Jane's eyes. There was a pause while each took stock of the other.

"You'll be Jane," stated the giant's wife, giving her hands a hasty wipe on the kitchen towel.

She advanced on Jane.

"Pleased to meet you, hen," she said.

The hand which she offered was large, red and damp, but the pressure was firm.

"I forgot to put ma wallies in the day; they're still on the mantelpiece."

Mrs. McSporran said this to everyone whom she met for the first time.

"Ma grandweans like me best this way. They're aye craikin' for me to put on ma Punch and Judy face as they cry it," she went on, drawing in her lips with a sudden suction which almost brought her nose and chin into contact.

This was her customary opening gambit with children and it never failed to take a trick. She laughed heartily, exposing her toothless gums and Jane laughed too. The ice was broken.

"Their other granny could dae the same if she liked," she continued, transferring a pile of Mr. Purdie's shirts to the spinner, "but she prefers to keep her wallies in. See ma man! He'll be sixty at his birthday and he's still got a' his ain teeth. They're like pearls."

She allowed the spinner to fill with water and sorted out the next tubful of washing.

"Ah lost a' mine efter oor Jenny was born," she reported conversationally.

The first tub rumbled into action on the household linen while the second spewed the rinsing water from the shirts into the sink.

"Jenny's ma youngest," said Mrs. McSporran, turning to Jane who had not yet divested herself of her coat and hat. Mrs. McSporran did not seem to need the usual responses from her listener in order to maintain the flow of her eloquence. "She's fell pregnant again. They were a' visitin' me last night. She's got an awfy guid man and two wee weans. Wee Hughie doesnie like me wearin' troosers. He says he canny sit on my knee so well. I havenie got a lap."

She laughed again.

In the course of the next twenty minutes, Jane was introduced to each of Mrs. McSporran's eight children, their respective spouses and offspring and the virtues and failings of each. Several, it transpired, had crossed the seas to settle in the furthermost outposts of the Commonwealth. There was even a granddaughter who, at sixteen, was proving herself a worthy scion of the McSporran line, being due to burgeon at any moment. Such a progeny, extending already into a third generation, was awe-inspiring evidence of Mrs. McSporran's fecundity, and Jane listened with due reverence. Like Sarah in the Bible, she was a mother of nations.

The magnificence of her motherhood increased still further in Jane's eyes when Mrs. McSporran revealed that after her own children no longer needed her, she had taken three foster-children, two boys and a girl.

"Does that mean you're a foster-mother?" asked Jane with great respect.

"Aye, it does," replied Mrs. McSporran, filling up the washtub for the last time. "I've reared thae wee weans since they were nothing at a'."

Jane went suddenly pink for she was not quite sure of the functions of a foster-mother. How did she feed the children she cared for? Her eyes strayed to Mrs. McSporran's generous unsupported bosom and she wondered if the three foster-children as well as the eight McSporrans had derived nourishment from the same source. Was that why she was so big—or was it because she was so big that she had had more than enough to go round? Already in Jane's eyes, the three unknown foster-children were united to the McSporran lineage by a mystical link provided by the matriarchal milk.

The completion of the washing brought Mrs. McSporran's eloquence to a halt.

"Tell your Da I'll do the ironing the morn," she said as she pushed the washing machine back against the wall. "I've got the hall carpet to hoover and then I'll away."

Fascinated though she had been by the McSporran saga, Jane was glad to make her escape into the living room, where she started her homework to the brassy accompaniment of the hoover and its intermittent banging against the skirting board. With the chiming of the half hour Mrs. McSporran did not have the time to be fastidious.

"I've got the weanses' tea to get ready," she explained as she put on her coat, "and I'm going to the Golden Age the night."

For Jane, the Golden Age held connotations of an ethereal world populated by Greek gods and Nordic heroes, and against this Mrs. McSporran seemed something of an incongruity. Her solid appearance, moreover, hardly suggested an early departure to another sphere. It appeared, however, that the Golden Age was the local Pensioners' Club where she had volunteered her services. So the old people too benefited from Mrs. McSporran's bounty!

"Ta-ta, hen," she said as Jane came to the door with her, and in a minute, she had vanished into the dusk.

Twenty to six. In half an hour Mr. Purdie would be home. Jane put the tablecloth on the table and went into the kitchen for the cups and saucers. She would make some macaroni and cheese.

Tea could be rather a silent meal in which both father and daughter tended to be absorbed in their own thoughts. George might or might not be watching the television but the continuing voice provided a cover behind which he could retreat, at least until his appetite was satisfied. The time for talking came afterwards.

"Did you get on all right at school today?" he asked when he had poured himself a last cup of tea.

Jane's eyes fell as she disclosed the incident of the ink-bottle, carefully omitting reference to the conversation which preceded it.

"I had done the exercise specially carefully because it was for Miss Chalmers," she concluded, tears welling up afresh. "And now it's all spoiled and she'll maybe not be able to read it."

The glimmer of a smile appeared on Mr. Purdie's face as he divined the significance of the remark.

"Hey, what's this?" he exclaimed. "I thought it was Miss Jackson that was your favourite."

"Well, it's Miss Chalmers now," said Jane with a soulful resignation. "I saw her playing hockey and when the rain started, she took me in and gave me shelter at the school. She let me help her set the tea out and she was so nice today when I spilled the ink."

Mr. Purdie sipped his tea. He had heard similar panegyrics on the subject of Miss Jackson's perfections and was amused by Jane's earnestness. He had not met Jane's teachers, and found some difficulty in extracting reality from her rhapsodies.

"Well, I think I prefer Miss Jackson," he replied with mock seriousness which made Jane smile in spite of herself. "I don't like women who play hockey."

"Oh, but you would like Miss Chalmers if you saw *her* playing," protested Jane. "She's *so* beautiful. You should see her doing that funny wee thing with her hockey stick when they're beginning again after a goal. Look, I'll show you. Take your teaspoon."

Some extra stains were added to the tablecloth as the two spoons tapped in miniature illustration of the bully-off.

Mr. Purdie laughed.

"But it's not so long since you discovered where Miss Jackson lived," he commented, "and you took a leaf from her hedge and a pebble from her path."

"I'll throw them away," said Jane loftily. "The leaf's fallen to bits anyway."

"Where did you keep them?" asked Mr. Purdie.

"In my trinket box along with my jewels," replied Jane.

Jane's jewels consisted of a broken necklace, a trinket from a Hallowe'en cake, a tooth, some shells, a bracelet which she never wore and a brooch which had belonged to her mother.

"Well, Miss Jackson's my favourite," said Mr. Purdie emphatically. He cupped his face with both hands and stared into space as he had seen Jane do so often. "There's no one quite like her."

Jane was quick to see the humour of the situation but pride demanded that he should be scolded.

She pushed at the elbow which was propped on the table.

"Oh, Daddy, you've not to go on like that," she remonstrated, trying without success to suppress her own laughter. "Miss Jackson was very nice but Miss Chalmers is nicer."

Mr. Purdie became quickly sober and returned to the day's problems.

"Why don't you do the exercise again tonight?" he suggested.

"But Miss Chalmers has got my exercise book," said Jane. "After she had blotted it up, she could just read what I'd written."

"You can do it on some spare paper," replied Mr. Purdie. "Then Miss Chalmers will see what it looked like before the ink spilled over it."

Jane looked doubtful.

"Maybe she'll think I'm fussing," she temporised.

"No, she won't," replied Mr. Purdie reassuringly. "I'll clear up and you can get started."

Five minutes later, Jane was hard at work redoing the exercise in her neatest writing.

***

The rewriting of the exercise drew the sting from the memory of the overturned ink-bottle and Jane faced the following day with renewed confidence. Indeed, she could not prevent the corners of her mouth creasing up into a smile, and it was only by dint of continually pursing her lips that she managed to keep her features under control. Madge and Fiona were mystified by this evidence of suppressed high spirits but Jane shook her head gleefully when they asked for the reason. Just for the present it was too private to share, this deliciously anticipated moment when she would step out from the body of the class, approach Miss Chalmers and deliver up her spotless offering.

Staff and girls assembled for prayers in the school chapel, a church building adjoining the school which had been acquired from the Trustees after a diminishing congregation had necessitated its closure. A connecting corridor had been built and it had served a useful purpose in accommodating the school at the daily morning assembly.

The hymn was announced; Miss Henderson, the music teacher, led the piano accompaniment and a trio of strings, on duty for the week from the school orchestra, swept into action.

Jane's pent-up emotions found release in singing. Her view of Miss Chalmers was partially obstructed by Angela Brown in the row in front, who was swaying from side to side, with head up-tilted, in affirmation of her fervour. With each alternate movement of Angela's head, Jane could see Miss Chalmers who was standing between Miss McTurk and Miss Mason in the transept. Her eyes dwelt lovingly on the curly hair and the finely pencilled brows, and she watched the lips earnestly framing the words of the well-known hymn. Surely, at that moment Miss Chalmers was in direct communication with the Almighty and was receiving from Him the love that she would later mediate to her pupils.

"To them that seek Thee Thou art good,

To them that find Thee, all in all," sang Jane with all her heart, keeping one finger on the place so that she might not miss the intermittent views of Miss Chalmers vouchsafed by the vibrating Angela.

"Our restless spirits yearn for Thee," continued the hymn. Jane's voice trembled with the strength of her feelings and Madge, who was at her side, turned to give her a knowing smile.

"Glad when Thy gracious smile we see."

The words were invested with meaning, precious if displaced, by one singer at least.

"Shed o'er the world Thy holy light."

Jane poured her very soul into the concluding lines, and took a last ecstatic peep round Angela's shoulder before staff and girls resumed their seats.

"That was blasphemy," whispered Fiona reprovingly.

Jane felt momentarily rebuffed but gathered her wits sufficiently to return the rebuke.

"Who stares at you in the Bible Class?" she hissed before giving her attention to the Bible reading from Miss Armstrong.

"Come now, and let us reason together, said the Lord: though your sins be as scarlet, they shall be as white as snow: though they be red like crimson they shall be as wool."

Miss Armstrong's bearing was dignified but her stern voice failed to convey the atoning message of the passage. She was not in agreement with the Lord, the incisive tone seemed to say.

Jane did not worry. She felt confident that Miss Chalmers, like Isaiah, would take the more lenient view. The blue ink-splash, like its scarlet counterpart, would be washed away.

The short service concluded with the Lord's Prayer which was reputedly recited in Latin by Miss Kelvin, Head of the Classics Department. As she occupied the rostrum along with the other principal teachers, however, no one was ever able to prove or disprove the rumour.

Meanwhile, there were mathematical morasses to be circumvented and grammatical hurdles to be taken, in tongues ancient and modern. The English class did not meet until the afternoon.

Lunch over, the girls returned to their classroom to assemble their books for afternoon lessons. Jane decided to make a last inspection of her rewritten exercise. She had put the single sheet of paper inside her Latin exercise book to keep it clean. She flipped it open. Horror of horrors, it was not there! She shook it by the covers but no immediate loose leaf fluttered out. With mounting anxiety, she inspected her other exercise books, then her textbooks, then the neatly arranged contents of her desk.

Nothing could be plainer. The rewritten exercise had vanished and with it went the elation of the morning.

She was so sure that she had put it into her Latin exercise book. Had it slipped out? In that case it would still be at home and could be retrieved—but not until tonight. Impossible to hurry home now and be back in time for Miss Chalmers at the half hour. Perhaps tomorrow the original exercises would be returned, corrected, and there would be little point in submitting what she had redone so meticulously. And she had wanted so much to earn Miss Chalmers' favour! Despair descended.

***

Mr. Purdie approached the school diffidently and conscience-stricken. He had been in it only twice before, first when he had made enquiries about enrolling Jane two years previously and again the following summer when he had taken a day's leave to attend prize giving.

It was his fault that the exercise had been left on the sideboard. After Jane had gone to bed, he had been unable to resist taking it from her schoolbag which had been left open, to enable her to see once again the neatness of her rewritten exercise. The telephone bell had rung, he had laid it down and it was not until the following day at lunch-time that a quick look-in on Mrs. McSporran had shown that it was still on the sideboard.

Despite the school's excellent endowment, fees were required and these constituted a heavy item in Mr. Purdie's expenditure. Initial doubts as to his capacity to meet them had been largely resolved by a decision to discontinue smoking to which he had become addicted since his wife's death. Impressed by the school's academic reputation and encouraged by Jane's progress, he had successfully overcome his craving for tobacco and the addiction to polo mints which followed. Elspeth had always wanted Jane to go to Earlswood and, thinking back to his own lack of educational opportunity, Mr. Purdie felt that it was money well spent.

Approaching the school-gate, he scanned the girls who were in the playground. No, Jane was not there. He hesitated before entering. Only once during term-time had he made direct contact with the school and that was when he had telephoned Miss Armstrong regarding a delay in the payment of the autumn instalment of fees. Her tone had been acid and had conveyed the impression to the apologetic Mr. Purdie that a great concession had been granted him through the admission of his daughter to the school—Jane, who had come third in her class last year!

He entered the school-hall and gazed about him, pleasantly awed by a majestic line of portraits of those who had held office of Headmistress since the inception of the school a hundred years previously, and the Gold Medallist Boards to which, over the years, the names of the Dux Girls had been inscribed in gold letters. Perhaps, one day, Jane's name would appear on the roll of honour!

He wondered where the Janitor was to be found and as he paused, uncertain what to do, a teacher, in academic gown, approached.

"Please forgive the intrusion," said Mr. Purdie in reply to her offer of assistance. "I am anxious that my daughter should have this exercise. It was inadvertently left at home."

He drew the sheet of exercise paper from his briefcase. Jane had written her name at the top.

The teacher smiled. She seemed anxious to help.

"Yes, I know Jane," she replied, "in fact, I'm on my way to her class now."

She scanned the exercise.

"There was no need for her to redo it," she said, shaking her head gently. "I hope she wasn't still distressed when she got home."

Her concern was genuine and she turned a mildly questioning look on Mr. Purdie who found himself relaxing in spite of himself. He too smiled.

"Are you Miss Chalmers?" he asked. "Well, yes, she was a bit upset. Everything she does has to be perfect. I'm a bit like that myself. It was my suggestion really—to do it again—but it seemed to suit her."

"I'm afraid her skirt was badly marked too," continued Miss Chalmers, "but I think Miss McBride dealt with that."

"Jane didn't mention her skirt," replied Mr. Purdie. "It was the exercise that bothered her. I—I hope she'll not lose any marks because of this—she's so keen to do well."

Miss Chalmers smiled again.

"Don't let that worry you, Mr. Purdie," she said reassuringly. "Jane is a most conscientious pupil."

***

Jane was agog that night and could hardly wait till Mr. Purdie arrived home. She hurried to the door on hearing the key turning in the lock.

At first, she could not find words to express the pleasure that surged through her with the awareness that she could now share her daily enthusiasms more intimately, but first she wanted confirmation that her treasure shone as brightly in her father's eyes as in her own. She needed his approval before she could grasp and possess that lofty identity with her idol which she had sought so earnestly.

There she stood in the middle of the hall carpet as Mr. Purdie crossed the threshold and, like the Cheshire cat, she could only smile and smile and smile.

Mr. Purdie knew his Jane. He was also rather pleased with himself for having helped to redeem the initial calamity as well as the subsequent error. He too wanted to shout aloud his gladness, but by a determined pursing of his lips, he endeavoured to restrain himself. Jane had seen that look many times and understood it. The little man knew he had earned his medals and wanted Jane to award them. The big man tried to brush the matter aside.

Jane's questions poured out in a torrent.

"How did you know it was Miss Chalmers? What did she say when she saw the exercise? Did you say who you were? Whereabouts did you see her? Did she say anything special about me? Isn't she really beautiful?"

Mr. Purdie struggled out of his coat and grappled with the questions.

"How did I know it was Miss Chalmers?" he repeated, still endeavouring to maintain his gravity. "Just because she was, as you've said, so beautiful. As soon as I saw her I said to myself, 'That must be Miss Chalmers'."

Jane knew he was teasing and tried unsuccessfully to be cross.

"Och, you did not," she answered. "Go on, tell me what really happened."

"Well, Jane," said Mr. Purdie, lighting the gas under the kettle, "it was really the other way round. When she saw what a good-looking chap I was she said, 'That must be Jane Purdie's father'."

There was a quality about his humour that Jane found irresistible, though she could not have analysed her feelings. This plain, ordinary, loveable man, who had an untiring faculty of turning cloud into sunshine, carried with him something of the aura of a Prince Charming. She loved his teasing but did not really know how to cope with it.

"Och, stop it, Daddy," she scolded. "Tell me what really happened."

And when the narration was completed, there was one last question.

"She really is wonderful, isn't she?"

Mr. Purdie considered thoughtfully before giving his answer.

"Yes, Jane, perhaps she is."

Chapter V
Miss Chalmers And Sports Day

To those whose acquaintance with her was not intimate, Alison Chalmers had been born with the proverbial silver spoon in her mouth. To a heritage of good looks and ability was added achievement, both scholastic and athletic. She had wide interests—amateur dramatics, dress-making, hill-walking, sketching—and through them she had made many friends.

In whatever activity she engaged, she showed to advantage, for her absorption was never less than total. To her pupils and colleagues, she appeared as the ideal teacher. Her equal as centre-forward was not to be found in local hockey. Equipped with haversack and walking-boots she displayed vigour and resource. At the sewing-machine she showed the application of a Penelope. With sketch-book and pencil she might have been a professional artist.

To her friends she was a splendid all-rounder. Only a few were aware that her self-sufficiency was more apparent than real.

As a teenager, some fifteen years previously, the shyness of early adolescence had loosened when developing womanhood had conferred on her the attention of most of the lads of the neighbourhood. Most of them went through an Alison Chalmers phase. She had known nothing of the personal uncertainties of the less attractive girl and she was quick to take advantage of masculine susceptibilities. Thus emancipated from her position at home as youngest of a large family, she enjoyed her power and flirted with a succession of boyfriends, without however becoming involved herself.

Then she met Alastair, a young houseman, and for the first time Alison knew what it was to be in love. Alastair, clever, ambitious, beauty-loving, was quick to respond to the attractive honours-year student and within months they were engaged. For Alison, it was the natural climax to a succession of relationships in which she had never known failure or rejection. She looked forward to marriage, to the children they would have, to the social position she would enjoy as wife to the consultant Alastair intended to become. The future seemed secure.

Alastair saw an opening in Aberdeen that would further his career. He applied for it and was accepted. A house was purchased. The wedding date was fixed. The reception was booked. Invitations were sent and presents rolled in.

Then misfortune intervened. Alison became involved in a car accident resulting in multiple fractures. Though the wedding was called off, the cloud was as yet no bigger than a man's hand. Dr. Alastair was optimistic. Time and medical treatment would bring their own therapy. Normal living would be resumed within a reasonable period and the wedding would follow. He wrote interesting sympathetic letters from Aberdeen, and from her hospital bed Alison regained hope and once again began to look forward to the future.

But the cloud grew larger when Alastair's letters became irregular, and it blotted out the sun when he at last wrote asking to be released from his engagement.

Recovery of physical health was followed by near breakdown. For some months, Alison's confidence deserted her. Her faith in everyone, family and friends alike, sustained a serious blow. For a time, she was afraid of meeting people and was unable to keep appointments. She felt herself disintegrating as a personality.

Slowly, she groped her way back to normality, completed her teacher training and started teaching.

Success with her pupils did much to restore her lost confidence. She took up hockey again and joined a sketching class.

Her parents breathed a sigh of relief.

"Alison's back to her old self again," they said.

She even resumed a friendship with an ex-boyfriend. Andy was overjoyed, being at first unaware that her acceptance of his overtures was based solely on the fact that she felt safe with him. There were no ecstasies in his company and after a few months she grew tired of him.

Then came the hill-walking holiday in the Lake District. It was there that she met Hector.

Hector came from the West Highlands but was living and working in Glasgow on a temporary footing. At first, his taciturnity was off-putting but gradually, she came to perceive an underlying sensitivity and found reassurance in his lack of sociability. By the end of the holiday, before she was aware of it, she was head over heels in love with him and he with her.

Once more swept away on a wave that she could not control, she continued to see him in Glasgow after the holiday. She felt happier than she had been since her engagement with Alastair had been broken off. She knew she would accept him if he proposed.

Then the axe fell. She learned from a friend that he was already married. When taxed, he acknowledged the fact and was obliged to confess that there was no question of divorce.

Alison never saw him again. She relived some of her earlier anguish and then appeared to come to terms with life again. She changed schools, moving from a junior post in a co-educational school to a promoted post at Earlswood Girls'. There was comfort in this world of women in whose society she felt peculiarly invulnerable. The demands made on her were exacting but they were of a professional nature and Alison eagerly accepted the challenge. She loved teaching and had a natural affinity with young people, to whom she readily exposed the warmer side of her nature. She willingly participated in extra-curricular activities and accompanied school parties on holidays and excursions.

The superstructure was strong but an occasional echo from the past sounding through the busy tenor of her life caused a tremor to shake the foundations. Alison was conscious of this, had accepted its inevitability but felt sufficiently entrenched in her chosen way of life to escape major upheaval.

***

With the approach of June came the hurdles of examination papers to be marked, report cards to be compiled, Sports Day and end of term concerts to be organised. The physical training staff was responsible for organising the Sports Day, but younger members of staff usually participated, and most of the teachers looked in at some part of the afternoon.

The events were held in the playing fields beside the school. Anxious faces smiled when a drizzly week gave way to clear skies and sunshine on Saturday morning.

From early on, girls and staff were at the field which quickly became the centre of happy activity. Markers for the various events were fixed in position, the track for the relay race was laid out, lemonade and ice-cream stalls were set up and bunting was raised around the awning where prizes were to be distributed.

At one end of the playing-field stood Miss Peters, the Principal Physical Education Teacher, in loose-fitting skirt and anorak, tall, slender and as agile at sixty as when the mothers of the present generation of Earlswood girls jumped the horse and shinned up the ropes thirty years previously. The day's arrangements were proceeding according to plans worked out in a series of meetings with her colleagues on the physical education staff and more recently with volunteers from the general teaching staff. The school was to be fully represented in the events— upper school, lower school, primary and infants. There would be senior and junior relay races, the mile, half mile, hundred yards, hurdles, high jump, long jump, and children's events such as the sack race, the three-legged race and egg-and-spoon race. Full participation was enjoined and the various heats had been run during the previous week.

"Let's hope we're better supplied with refreshments this year," murmured Miss Chalmers who was organising the sweets and lemonade stall. "We ran out before the first hour was over last year."

"Don't forget Patsy Pratt has left school since then," replied Miss McTurk with a laugh. "She wasn't competing and she hardly moved from the refreshment stall."

"Yes, but her sister Lottie is just like her," rejoined Miss Chalmers. "If Lottie comes, she'll probably bring Patsy with her and that means we'll have two of them."

"Don't worry, ladies," called Miss Peters reassuringly in passing. "We've ordered double supplies this year. That's the delivery van now."

With the approach of noon contestants and their parents began to arrive. Both sides of the street and those adjoining were soon flanked with cars, parked nose to tail. Faces began to appear at the windows of the tenement buildings which overlooked two sides of the field and passers-by stopped to have a peep through the fence. Sports Day always attracted local notice. Mr. Jamieson, the janitor, had brought up a supply of folding chairs from the school building and a team of senior girls had arranged these around the grassy verges.

Miss Peters' voice sounded at intervals over the amplifier, directing participants to their respective starting-lines. The report of a pistol intermittently announced the start of the various races and alternated with the cheers of encouragement and congratulations that rose on all sides as the events got underway. The parental clap was also to be heard, though less loudly. Enthusiasm ran high both among the contestants and spectators. Cameras clicked constantly. The sun blazed down from a cloudless sky. The queue for lemonade and ice-cream remained steady and there was a continual stream of mothers and younger children to the toilets at either end of the school building, discreetly divided between the sexes for the occasion.

Madge won the hundred yards for her year and Jane came third. Angela Brown, press-ganged as a last-minute replacement into the relay race, did her willing best for the honour of the class but co-ordination between brain and limbs was somehow lacking, and the legs which gave promise of height failed to respond to the shrieking exhortations of her classmates.

"I don't know what we're going to do with that girl," sighed Miss Moir, the young assistant Physical Education teacher, as Angela collapsed exhausted at the post, having successfully converted what promised to be honourable mention into a dismal final place for the team.

"Oh, her schoolwork's not bad," countered Miss Mason who, like Angela, had never been noted for her agility.

Miss Moir, whose scholastic record had not been of the best, snorted.

"What's the good of that if she can't control her own body?" she retorted.

Athletic senior girls made good showing in the high and long jumps. Most had been practising for weeks and the dimensions cleared were creditable.

"Well done, Karen," cried Miss Peters to a tall, well-made girl who landed on the sand at her feet. Karen bid fair to be sports champion and intended to proceed to the Physical Training College in the autumn.

Relay races complete, the contestants for the mile assembled at the starting line. Sack-racers stumbled laughingly to the winning-post; well-practised three-legged runners trotted neatly in; eggs changed spoons and were near to being scrambled by their scrambling bearers. Parents dispensed crisps alike to weeping losers and complacent victors.

Miss McPhail, who had been holding one end of the finishing tape for the three-legged race, rearranged her hair pins to prevent disaster befalling her neatly braided hair. It was hotter than she liked. Had she been at home she would either have been indoors or sitting in the shady part of her garden, but the younger pupils ran better when someone they knew was at the winning-post. She really preferred her neatly marching school class to this apparently amorphous activity in the open air.

George Purdie had arrived at the playing-field with Jane shortly after the first events had started, and had amused himself in desultory fashion strolling up and down the field. He was selective in his sociability. The tenor of his life following marriage and widowhood had not been such as to foster the sociable side of his nature, and he had accepted the limitations of his sequestered existence, had even come to enjoy it as a mole does its hole. He shrank from crowds, especially a crowd of this kind which seemed intent on playing a never-ending game of Happy Families, thrusting its cheerful domesticity aggressively upon the lone paterfamilias. At such times, he found himself unreasonably irritated by the presence of other men's wives and looked, usually in vain, for a kindred spirit of his own sex. He would frequently break into chat with some congenial-looking fellow, to find that the casual camaraderie of one man with another was only too quickly disturbed by the arrival of the latter's good lady.

Jane's participation was the sole reason for his appearance. He had watched her tearing eagerly through the hundred yards, her performance marred by her uncertain getaway and by her anxious side-glances at the other contestants as she ran. Jane was like himself. She had a need to excel and competition created anxiety. He sighed, hardly knowing whether to be thankful or regretful that time had blunted his own aspirations.

The comparative anonymity of the relay race had brought a relaxation of tension. Honours having fallen to IC, Mr. Purdie sought his daughter and found her at the centre of a gaggle of classmates who were roundly berating the unfortunate Angela Brown.

"Why didn't you lift your legs?"

"We would have won if it hadn't been for you."

"We were shouting and shouting and shouting and you didn't hear us!"

Fortunately for Angela, her emotional reactions were no quicker than her physical reactions, and having regained her breath, she smoothed her hair and defended herself placidly against her vociferous assailants.

"I don't know what you're complaining about. *I* didn't ask to go into the relay team. *You* made me do it. *You* pushed me into it."

Mr. Purdie hovered on the outskirts of the little group which seemed bent on lynching its press-ganged victim. He had observed Angela's gallant but unavailing effort on the track and was glad when the girls began to drift away.

"What about an ice-cream, Jane?" he suggested to his daughter, whose face was flushed from exertion and excitement.

Jane, still in gym blouse and knickers, willingly complied. She wanted something cooling and had early taken note that Miss Chalmers, with two senior girls, was officiating at the refreshment stall. They took their place in the queue.

"There's Miss Chalmers," she whispered to her father, her heart thudding every bit as fast as when she had contested the hundred yards.

The presiding staff had had a constant job, for the refreshment stall had been well patronised. Miss Chalmers was putting a fresh consignment of Toffee Bars on the table that served as a counter and added the previously emptied box to a growing pile in the rear. There was a smile of welcome for Jane and her father.

"Well, Jane, have you won any cups?"

Jane's hot face became even hotter with the thrill of informal contact.

"Good afternoon, Miss Chalmers," said Mr. Purdie, raising his cap. It was a dying courtesy to which he adhered from long habit. He had learned it at the age of seven or so, not from his parents but from his class teacher, a stout, kindly spinster lady, who had instructed the boys on the importance of social etiquette. He remembered how, in company with a cluster of little boys, he had stood at the school gate before afternoon school to greet Miss Lightbody with the appropriate salutation.

There was a hesitant raising of hands to caps, the bolder ones nudging the others into action. He still recalled her smile of pleasure in noting the children's compliance.

"Good afternoon, Mr. Purdie," replied Miss Chalmers. "I think it's been almost as warm for the spectators as for the girls."

"And for the staff at the refreshment stall," returned Mr. Purdie. "You've had a busy afternoon."

Miss Chalmers laughed in agreement.

"We picked the shadiest part of the field," she said, "to keep the ice-cream cool but it's been pretty hot all the same, hasn't it, girls?"

She referred to her two young assistants who indicated their agreement.

In spite of the heat, Miss Chalmers herself had managed to preserve a cool, unruffled exterior but she leaned momentarily against the table as though for support.

Mr. Purdie was quick to notice.

"Have you sampled your own wares yet, Miss Chalmers?" he asked. "Perhaps you'll let me swell the funds by having an ice on me—and your assistants, of course," he added hastily.

Miss Chalmers nodded a smiling acquiescence.

"Come along, Stella," she said to one of the senior girls. "Forward to the counter, please!"

Stella and Margaret gratefully complied. There was a temporary lull in business and all five enjoyed a much-needed cooler.

Jane had a delightful consciousness of belonging to this temporarily formed grouping. It was as though a number of particles floating aimlessly through space had suddenly formed a fortuitous but meaningful combination. Despite her friendship with Madge and Fiona, Jane's social experience had tended to be peripheral, but at this moment she had an acute awareness of herself as an integral part of the afternoon's proceedings. She could not have explained her heightened sensibilities—she heard the casually murmured conversation between her father and Miss Chalmers against a background of schoolgirl acclamations; she felt the warmth of the June sun hot on her head and through her blouse and on the back of her legs; and, in contrast, the cooling balm of the ice-cream on her tongue and as it slipped down, down, down; she was aware of the two older girls participating in her father's bounty and exchanging sporadic comments on the races. Their seniority gave Jane added status.

Suddenly, the diminishing ice-cream was no more and something of the magic departed. Jane rubbed her sticky hands on her bare thighs. It was strangely delightful to see her father and Miss Chalmers chatting together as though they had always known each other. She wanted to listen to their conversation but felt it more appropriate to turn and watch the remaining events. But her thoughts were wholly absorbed by these two all important figures, whom she could just see out of the corner of her eye. She found herself considering each from the standpoint of the other—her father, square, solid, reliable, a brown forearm showing from the casually rolled-up blue-checked sleeve—surely, Miss Chalmers must find him handsome! Miss Chalmers, lovely beyond compare, smiling, animated. How wonderful to be able to compare notes with her father later on. Perhaps he would envy her daily proximity to such a beautiful lady.

A prolonged blast of Miss Peters' whistle announced the end of the sports and there was a general move in the direction of the presentation platform.

"Come on, Jane," said Mr. Purdie shepherding his daughter downfield. "You don't want to be too far away when your name's called."

***

And suddenly, it was all over. Jane had received a book token which she had given into her father's safe keeping and they were making their way out of the field.

But it was not all over—quite. The dismantling process had already begun by girls and staff previously appointed to the task. Jane turned to take a last lingering look at the refreshment stall. The janitor had already conveyed the table away. Stella and Margaret between them were moving a sackful of empty cardboard boxes and what little remained of unsold stock. Miss Chalmers was standing by the ice-cream container.

By coincidence, Mr. Purdie was also looking in that direction. His eyes met Jane's.

"Come on, Jane, let's help Miss Chalmers," he suggested.

Jane did not need to be asked twice.

There was a smiling protest from Miss Chalmers—Stella and Margaret would soon be back—or Mr. Jamieson—or Miss Peters—or... Why should she be so reluctant to accept her father's assistance, Jane wondered. He was so strong and so willing. With her eyes, she beseeched Miss Chalmers to say Yes. Would not this forge an unbreakable link between her idol and herself! Miss Chalmers would see Jane as the willing daughter of the willing father who helped her with the ice-cream container, and the rest of Jane's school life would be spent basking in her favour. Plea-ea-se, Miss Chalmers.

The unspoken plea was heard and Miss Chalmers did indeed comply.

"If you insist," she said with a little laugh.

Jane wanted to hug herself. What a wonderful day it had been, even more wonderful than the day when the rain had stopped hockey play. On that day Miss Chalmers had asked who all lived at home. Now, she had met and spoken with her father and they had all had ice-cream together.

With the return of the container, farewells were exchanged and Mr. Purdie and Jane proceeded to drive home. Jane's cup was full to overflowing and she made no attempt to contain herself. She was so full of love and happiness that she needed no response to the ecstatic utterances which poured from her in an uninterrupted torrent.

"She's so beautiful, isn't she, Daddy?" so ran the monologue. "D'you know, I was wanting to go to the refreshment stall all afternoon—not really for refreshments but just because Miss Chalmers was there.

She looked so pretty in that flowery dress, didn't she? She's got a lovely smile. One of her front teeth crosses over the other, did you notice? I like her hair. It's naturally curly. I wish mine were like that."

Mr. Purdie made no comment. He had heard it all before when Miss Jackson had held prime place in Jane's affections. He had teased her affectionately then but now he was silent. Jane was too wound-up to notice.

"I love everything about her," she went on. "I love her face, I love her eyes, I love her voice, I feel so happy when she looks at me. I can't wait until Monday to see her again. We get her first two periods in the morning."

Mr. Purdie maintained his silence as he drove along but he noted every word. Perhaps there was comfort in listening to this paean of praise which he would have been unable to utter himself, but which he echoed in his heart. It was foolishness, he told himself, for he did not intend to take the matter further, but it was a foolishness that made him lift his head and straighten his shoulders and brought him such an influx of joy that he wanted to shout Hallelujah!

Jane's eloquence continued unabated. Her prattle was the next best thing to being with the enchantress herself.

"I'm sure you'll change your mind about women playing hockey now," said Jane. "I'm going to take it up myself after the holidays. I'll never be as good as she is but if I do what she does, I'll feel nearer her. She's good at everything and oh, she's so beautiful! She's the most beautiful person I've ever seen."

There was a certain lack of variety in Jane's soliloquy but Mr. Purdie did not seem to object.

"I wrote a poem about her once," said Jane. "Listen."

The engine of the car purred accompaniment as Jane's overtaxed emotions found fuller expression in the recitation of her own verse.

"Oh, gracious lady, fair and sweet,
I lay my heart down at your feet.
Lady so beautiful and dear,
Your lilting voice I love to hear,
Lady adored, O may I be
Forever pleasing unto thee.
Lady supreme, what power on earth
Could tear me from thy sterling worth
Which makes my heart's love blossom forth!"

Chapter VI
End Of Term

It was the end of July—thirty-two days after prize-giving when school closed down for the summer holidays. Thirty-two crosses on the calendar bore witness to thirty-two days in the wilderness. After prize-giving, a sober Jane had faced the reality that no fewer than sixty-two days must elapse before life could again have meaning. The days had stretched out in front of her like a desert. Even the prospect of her fortnight's holiday in August did not bear the semblance of a mirage.

As the June days had slipped away, she had been aware of the approaching gulf. Its inevitability she had accepted. Twelve months previously, the situation had not arisen with the same intensity. Then, as at every school holiday since her mother's death, there had been a certain sense of interruption in the continuity of life. This year, however, she had felt it more acutely on account of her developing emotional life, and the fact that these emotions had found a focus within the school.

Arrangements for Jane's care by neighbours or the mothers of friends or at the home of the current daily had worked with varying degrees of success. Jane liked best to be at the home of Madge, whose mother was youthful and unhurried and the days had been filled with dolls or marbles or ropes or exciting games of hide-and-seek. But the Stevensons' holidays did not always coincide with the Purdies' and this July they were going to a relative's farmhouse in the country.

Fiona's mother was well-meaning but her benevolence had an egotistic basis, and did not really extend beyond the needs of her own family whom she saw as an extension of herself. It was easier for Jane to play at Fiona's during term-time when no special demands were likely to be made on Mrs. Ross.

During the last few weeks, she had alternated between the immediate neighbours—Mrs. Gray, who had no children and who had always had a soft spot for Jane; Mrs. Maclean, whose children were much younger than Jane and did not provide much companionship; and Mrs. Hartley, who was kind but fussy and with whose daughter Jane did not always get on well.

With the thirty-second day, however, Jane's sun had reached and passed its winter solstice and her heart grew lighter with the knowledge that every passing day now brought her nearer to that mellow autumn season when her own personal sun would have reached its zenith.

In anticipating the long school holiday, Jane had known from her experience of shorter separations that the fortitude with which she would face it would depend entirely on the nature of her final contact with Miss Chalmers. If a warm smile gave Jane a special sense of Miss Chalmers' approval, she knew that she could venture forth, upheld by its memory, into a wilderness which would indeed blossom like the rose. If, on the other hand, the greeting in playground or corridor had less than the required degree of reassuring warmth, she knew that she would wander thirsting, like another Hagar, in a desert wherein no streams flowed.

Jane had done well in the end of term exams in which a little knot of girls vied with each other for top position in each subject and for the first few places overall. At the Christmas examinations Madge had topped the class in English, Jane in Mathematics, with Fiona runner-up in each. Sandra Morris had come first in both French and Latin with Madge and Jane hot on her heels. In Science and Art Jane had lagged sadly behind but had compensated by good marks in History and Geography. She had been third overall while Madge had led the class.

With the transfer of her affections from Miss Jackson of the Maths Department to Miss Chalmers of the English Department, Jane had aspired to outshine Madge, and with Miss Chalmers as form teacher assembling all the marks had hoped to be top overall, with sufficient marks to enable her to make up the Christmas leeway and top the class for the year.

In the race for the top it was not unknown, however, for the ambitious half-mark hunter (a term of Miss Caskie's coining) a-tremble at her own daring, politely to point out that the addition of the neat blue-pencilled figures on the test paper was a whole half-mark short, the new total transforming a humiliating tenth place to an entirely creditable ninth equal. There was many a teacher's headshake in the direction of these triumphant young ladies, who had invested their current value in a vulgar fraction.

Miss Kelvin, Principal Teacher of Classics, entered the classroom with the stateliness of a Roman matron and greeted the class appropriately.

"Salvete, puellae meae!"

The response was chanted in unison.

"Salve, O magistra!"

And the lesson began, exam papers were returned with comments, cheerful as well as candid.

"Well done, Angela, you've got the passive voice right at last. Perhaps you know now what it is to be loved, mmh?"

And she smiled affably over her spectacles. To love and to be loved was a concept as vital within the Latin class as in the world at large.

"Hands are clever, therefore feminine," she observed as she moved back and forward through the classroom.

Miss Kelvin was an ardent feminist. She was of even temperament but the older girls joked that her mood could be gauged by the angle of the hairpins which kept her bun in place.

A rebuke at full throttle was directed at one young lady.

"Stop screwing up your brows! You'll be paying hundreds of pounds one day to have these lines removed."

"Sandra, ninety-three, and Jane with ninety-six. Very good, indeed," said Miss Kelvin with a nod of approval.

"We wondered who would say 'Prima sum', do you remember? —and now we know."

Yes, she had been top overall in the May exams, second for the year with Madge first—steady, level-headed Madge who had not preened herself as Sandra or Fiona might have done, and who made Jane feel like the real victor when she said:

"Your marks are really much better than mine, Jane. It's just that you can't draw and I can."

Madge's father was an architect.

George attended prize-giving as he had attended the school concert two weeks previously. The concert had had a mixed programme consisting of choir and orchestral work, solo items and two sketches. Jane was a member of the choir and had a tiny walk-on part in one of the sketches.

The parents attended in large numbers and the evening was considered a resounding success.

George waited for his daughter outside the school where he had parked his car. Most of the other cars had dispersed but he knew that Jane would be a little late since, with the rest of the caste, she would require to change and remove her make-up.

Ah, there she was emerging from the playground. He held the door open.

"A splendid evening," he commented.

This was what Jane wanted him to say. But suddenly, she had caught sight of a familiar registration plate on the car parked immediately in front.

"Daddy, that's Miss Chalmers' car," she exclaimed. "She's not away yet. Oh, let's wait and see her."

Mr. Purdie smilingly shook his head.

"We can't do that, Jane," he replied. "It's getting late and Miss Chalmers may be some time yet if she's helping."

Jane clasped her hands beseechingly.

"But if it's not too late for her, it can't be too late for us," she protested. She gasped suddenly.

"Look, she's just coming!"

Two pairs of eyes were drawn towards the approaching figure. A mid-summer dusk was only just closing in and the air was soft and still. Within the car, silence possessed both father and daughter. With unhurried step Miss Chalmers drew nearer, unaware that she was being observed. Away from the brightly lit school building, she sought the refreshment of the cooling night air, doubly satisfying after the evening's exertions.

She drew the car key from her bag and unlocked the door. Jane was beside herself.

"Oh, Daddy, she hasn't seen us," she whispered. "Can't you sound your horn?"

Mr. Purdie shook his head.

"No, Jane," he replied very slowly. Jane stared.

"Well, let's drive after her," she suggested. "Maybe we'll find she goes part of our way."

Again Mr. Purdie shook his head. He stroked Jane's hair.

"Jane, dear," he said, and there was a serious note in his voice, "we must give Miss Chalmers the time and the freedom to go whichever way she chooses."

A sudden depression fell on Jane and the joy of the evening faded. She sensed, without understanding why, that a barrier stood between her father and herself on the one hand, and Miss Chalmers on the other, and that they must not attempt to cross it. The unalloyed pleasure of observing Miss Chalmers' approach now became tainted in her mind, and she had to suppress an inexplicable impulse to burst into tears. Silence again fell on father and daughter while Miss Chalmers entered her car, and it continued while she started the ignition and pulled away. It was still there during the few minutes which elapsed before Mr. Purdie drove off. All the way home it continued, and into the lock-up, into the house, till Jane was undressed and ready for bed.

She looked searchingly at her father.

"Goodnight, Daddy," she said.

A warmer smile than usual helped to revive Jane's spirits.

"Goodnight, Jane," responded Mr. Purdie. "It's been a wonderful evening."

And suddenly, it seemed that they had emerged from a rather frightening tunnel, where strange cross currents of electricity had converged on Jane and had shocked her into a paralysed silence. But everything was all right again, more than all right. She had done her part well; the evening had been a great success and Miss Chalmers had looked like an angel in the twilight.

But the feeling returned on prize-giving day when Jane, alone with her father after the ceremony and proud of the book under her arm, looked anxiously around the crowds of assembled parents for what must be a last glimpse of Miss Chalmers before the long holiday.

"Well, Jane, shall we go?" asked her father.

"I'm—I'm just wanting to say goodbye to all my friends," quavered Jane forlornly, barely returning the greeting of several girls passing by.

Mr. Purdie seemed restless.

"Well, you've said goodbye to quite a few of them," he replied with a shade of impatience in his voice. "Remember, I've booked a table at the hotel and we don't want to be late."

The crowd in front of Jane opened momentarily to give both of them a glimpse of Miss Chalmers with Madge's parents.

"Yes, please, please, Daddy," begged Jane, "I must say goodbye to Miss Chalmers. I won't see her again until September and it's such a long time."

Mr. Purdie yielded and an eternity of waiting began while the Stevensons retreated only to be replaced by first one couple, then another, and then Mr. Purdie found himself in conversation with Madge's parents.

At long last, Miss Chalmers became disengaged and looked around her, unhurried as usual. Her eyes met those of Mr. Purdie and Jane who waited for the usual kindly smile of welcome. It didn't come and it seemed to Jane as though there was a momentary vacuum when nothing had registered—or had something registered too much?

Her father filled an embarrassing pause.

"Good afternoon, Miss Chalmers," he greeted with his customary quiet affability. "You must be glad to have come to the end of another busy year."

There was a smiling acknowledgement; a word of praise for Jane's schoolwork which fell gratefully on Jane's ears. Some remarks were exchanged on the morning's ceremony, the standing of the school, the devotion of the staff, the good weather, the concert... Jane listened enthralled. It was like an echo of the Sports Day. It gave her a cosy feeling to think that she and Daddy and Miss Chalmers all liked one another.

Now Daddy was wishing Miss Chalmers an enjoyable holiday. There was a handshake, a long look, and suddenly Miss Chalmers was gone, and the special smile that Jane had waited for had vanished along with her.

***

July passed somehow. For the first time in her short life, Jane knew a sense of total isolation. The arms which had comforted her at the time of her mother's death were no longer offered as a haven. The sustaining element in the relationship with her father had gone. The sensitivity with which her every need had been anticipated appeared to have become blunted. The mother-father bird whose broad wings had given reassurance to the timid fledgling had withdrawn, and the fledgling felt itself to be plummeting down into a chasm of emptiness.

Where was the teasing comment, the cuddle, the patient audience, the willing self-immolation which had never yet been wanting? For the first week after prize-giving Jane was immersed in silent misery, which precluded a conscious awareness of the change in her father. She felt strangely inhibited from confiding in him but with a word of encouragement would gladly have poured her heart out.

The introjected father reminded her of the hockey-tea, the excellence of her school report, the shared ice-cream on the sunny but now remote Sports Day and a dozen other incidents, which should have reassured Jane of the affectionate regard in which Miss Chalmers held her, but the real father was silent and the daughter could not be comforted.

"Whit's wrang wi' ye, hen?" Mrs. McSporran had asked when Jane's downcast face had presented itself two days running. Jane had hesitated before uncovering the cause of her anguish, conscious of the disparity between Mrs. McSporran's action-packed life and her own.

Reddening, she confided her anxiety.

"I really can't help loving her," she concluded tearfully. Then, feeling that she must justify herself before Mrs. McSporran's astonished gaze, she added:

"My friend Madge loves Miss Jackson, the Maths teacher. I used to love Miss Jackson too but Miss Chalmers is much nicer."

Mrs. McSporran's approach to life was essentially practical, and the hothouse atmosphere of a girls' school, as suggested by Jane's anecdote, was beyond her experience.

"Well, if you'll take my advice, hen," she had responded sagely, "you'll forget a' aboot this Miss Chalmers and enjoy your holiday. She could easy have gave you a smile if that was what you wantit. It's just a pity you're no a year or two older and I would have tellt you to go and get yourself a lad." Mrs. McSporran pronounced it 'lod'.

"I'll never forget my first boyfriend," she went on reminiscently. "He lived up the next close…"

But Jane did not wait to hear the rest and slipped out. Half an hour later, in the late afternoon sunshine, she circled moodily around on her bicycle on a quiet intersection near the house. She watched her elongated shadow projecting inwards to the centre of the crossroads, foreshortening and lengthening alternately, now elliptical, now disproportionately large. It was monotonous but there was nothing else to do. Madge was on holiday and she was too engulfed in an emotional morass to be able to initiate social contact with anyone else. Books there were in plenty in the house but at that moment she had not the remotest interest in reading. Round and round she went, mesmerised by the motion, trailing her inner foot on the hot tarmac till further pedalling was needed to maintain movement.

Suddenly, George appeared further down the road on his way home from the office and she returned his wave. Then, leaving the orbit on which she had been travelling compulsively, she swung out on to the gradient leading past their home and free-wheeled downhill to meet him. A warm breeze ruffled her hair.

She was vaguely aware as she wheeled round to cycle slowly at his side that the absorption with his own thoughts no longer claimed him, and his smile of greeting brought an answering smile from her.

"What a warm afternoon it has been, Jane," he said, removing his hat from a forehead that was damp with perspiration. "What do you say to tea at the Millwheel? I fancy a change tonight."

And with that things fell once more into place.

Chapter VII
The Caravan In The Glen

The Glen Caravan Site was pleasantly secluded two miles away from the main road with which it was connected by a well surfaced country lane with open fields on either side. The lane crossed a bridge over a stream, circled round a little clump of woodland and entered the Caravan Park. It was small by comparison with other sites in the vicinity, accommodating twenty caravans only. The proprietor, a business man who had opted out of city life, lived on the site in a small white-washed cottage, formerly a farm worker's dwelling. A dry-stone dyke, in good repair, divided the cottage garden from the field beyond, in which the caravans were drawn up on three sides.

Tom Douglas had been in business now for six years and took pride in the efficient running of the site. He liked his nomadic friends and his stroll round their vans of an evening, taking orders personally for milk, rolls and eggs. During the daytime, he would tend his own garden or cut the grass on the site whether it needed cutting or not. He believed in making his presence unobtrusively felt. To the caravanners, he was a well-remembered figure and already he could count on a fair proportion of regulars.

He had been a colleague of Alison's older brother, Peter, who had shaken his head a few times when Tom had announced his intention of leaving the firm and starting afresh in a rural area. Initially uncertain as to the nature of the projected enterprise, he had finally decided in favour of a caravan site. Peter, to whom the whole idea of a do-it-yourself holiday had been at first unappealing, was now himself the enthusiastic owner of a caravan and, with his wife, had visited the Glen on more than one occasion. He shook his head now at the thought of his own whirlwind business life in Glasgow, willingly acknowledging that perhaps Tom had made the best bargain.

For Alison, the experience of caravanning was entirely new but, having spent a couple of weekends away with Peter and Ruth, she had decided to acquire a small caravan of her own.

The drive from Glasgow had been uneventful. Having already enjoyed a number of six-wheeler weekends, Alison was well accustomed to the sensation of towing, and had been amused when Maisie McTurk felt compelled from time to time to look round in order to confirm the following presence of their attachment. In the car mirror Alison could see the permanent reflexion of the silently rolling giant in the rear, and its restrictive pull made her conscious of the slightest gradient. The subsidiary roads with their rural charm and scenic grandeur had been studiously avoided and the route northwards had been mostly by arterial roadway.

A painted signboard gave advance notice of the Caravan Park, and Alison slowed before making a cautious wide turning into the lane.

"The day I bought the caravan I nearly took the lamp-post at the gate into the garden along with me," she recalled ruefully, "and it's made me wary of corners ever since."

They stopped outside Tom Douglas's cottage to announce their arrival.

"I've put you at Pitch No.5," he told them when the greetings were completed. "Peter likes it there. You'll get a fine view of Ben Riach from your back window."

The two young women surveyed the site with interest. Maisie had never caravanned before and the novelty of the situation made a strong appeal.

A dozen or so caravans were already positioned round three sides of the field, and Alison's caravan was to fill one of the remaining gaps. It was late afternoon but the sun still cast its steady warmth on little clusters of reclining sunbathers. Alison noted the usual wide range of caravan enthusiasts—the young, the not so young and those who were now past middle age. The great outdoors had beckoned to them all and the invitation had been accepted. On a day like this, however, most of them, having already abandoned traditional brick and mortar security, chose to detach even from the slender protection afforded by a caravan's aluminium walls and had surrendered themselves to summer with all the accompanying paraphernalia—garden loungers, folding chairs and windbreaks, whose floral patterns and sharp gay stripes vied with each other for brightness.

Racquets in hand, two teenagers were tossing a shuttlecock to and fro. A young man supported an infant who was taking his first few tottering steps. Two little girls busily pushed their prams up and down. One van was having its windows washed by an elderly woman in an apron, not quite able even on holiday, to abandon her housewifely role.

Despite the numbers, there was an air of tranquillity which Alison registered with satisfaction. Much as she loved the stir of school-life, she preferred a holiday which provided a complete contrast.

Carefully, she positioned the caravan, lowered the jockey wheel, the four legs and unhitched the van from the car.

She unlocked the door and made way for her friend. The caravan was small, not quite ten feet in length, and displayed characteristic compactness. There were two opposite facing settees with a table between them at one end and a long window seat at the other. On one side was a unit containing sink and cooking grill with cupboards above and below. On the other side, beside the door, was a little narrow wardrobe. The windows with their sunny chintz curtains radiated a quiet welcome. It was incredibly neat.

Maisie was enchanted.

"It's just like a doll's house," she enthused. "Oh, Alison, it's lovely."

A puzzled expression crossed her face.

"But where do we both sleep?"

Alison laughed.

"I'm not worried," grinned Maisie. "You can have the window-seat and I'll sleep outside."

She glanced across at the figures on the garden-loungers.

"I might have company!"

Alison laughed again.

"You'll not have to do that, Maisie," she replied. "The table folds down to the level of the settees, we slide the seat cushions across and the back cushions down—et voilà!—a double bed."

She did not demonstrate but Maisie followed her description.

"The brochure says it sleeps three-stroke-four," went on Alison. "Two in the double bed, one in the single, and the fourth—"

"Has a stroke!" Maisie could not resist that one.

More laughter.

"The fourth sleeps on a stretcher attached to these wall fittings," explained Alison. "It's an optional extra. But you can have the double bed, Maisie. You'll probably be happier if you can stretch a bit."

Maisie was taller than Alison.

"There are chores to be done before we can eat," Alison went on. "I told you we would be busy."

She reversed the car into position alongside the caravan and together they set to. The footstep and the pedal bin had to be set in position outside the door, the towel rail suspended from the back window and the slop pail placed strategically to catch the water as it drained from the miniature sink. There were the water containers to be filled from a tap only a few yards away. Finally, a mirror was placed on a shelf above the table.

"We're in business, Maisie," said Alison with an air of satisfaction.

Maisie collapsed on the settee in mock exhaustion.

But there were fresh delights for her inspection. Alison slid back the door of the little cupboard above the sink. A number of saucers and plates slithered out, detached from their moorings by the journey. Evading Alison's grasp, they clattered to the floor.

"Don't worry, nothing's breakable," said Alison to her amused friend. "This gorgeous Bakelite crockery is our tea set, to be tried out presently."

Further along the shelf stood an assortment of lidded containers acquired, willy-nilly, at an earlier date as free offers with various grocery products.

"We didn't need them at home," said Alison, "because Mother already had everything and they sat on the shelves getting covered with dust."

"And you really bought the caravan so that you could put them to use," Maisie chipped in.

"How did you guess?"

They both laughed.

She displayed two attractive butter dishes, one with a blue cover, the other cherry-coloured.

"Not that we need two," she said apologetically, "but we can put cheese in the other one."

Her eyes danced.

"Blue for butter, cherry for cheese, don't forget!"

Two little dumpy biscuit barrels came next, one with a variegated blue pattern, the other red.

"Blue for shoogar!" murmured Alison. "The red one's the tea-caddy."

Maisie spluttered.

Alison waved professionally towards the sink which held two plastic basins, yellow and blue, one inside the other.

"I can't wait to hear which is which," gasped Maisie.

Alison was momentarily unable to continue. Maisie's humour was infectious and for some moments, the two friends rocked in silent laughter. Oh, it was good!

"Mother got these some years ago with soap powder," Alison replied. "She didn't need either of them but she bought two packets all the same."

"And you don't need them either, at least not both," teased Maisie.

"We do the dishes in the yellow one," explained Alison. "The blue one—oh, dear, dare I say it?—is the blue-for-ablutions basin if there's too much of a crush in the Ladies'!"

Maisie rocked again.

"It's well seen you're a teacher, Alison," she said at length. "Blue for butter, blue-for-ablutions! I don't know! Well, what's on the me-n-u, and let me help."

Later on, Maisie washed up the plastic dinner-set with its delicately pastel-shaded plates. She was already in love with the caravan and found that even the washing-up was invested with its own peculiar charm.

"It's like playing houses, Alison," she said.

They sat at the little table in silent enjoyment of the mellow evening air, taking pleasure in surveying the activities of their fellow caravanners. The garden-loungers had been vacated and there was now no sign of small children. A new set of badminton enthusiasts flicked the shuttlecock to and fro. Tom Douglas was doing his rounds. An elderly couple from the next caravan were exercising their dog.

"Candy! Candy!" called the wife.

Alison smiled mischievously.

"Do you think they might be Mr. and Mrs. Floss?" she queried.

"Careful," warned Maisie, "you might call them that by mistake."

"I think we're going to be lucky with our neighbours," said Alison. "Mr. and Mrs. Floss seem nice and quiet and the family on the other side look well-behaved. Tom Douglas says there are to be more arrivals tomorrow."

Outside there was a hush broken only by the chirping of birds in the nearby trees. The evening air, cooling though still balmy, wafted in through the open door and windows. Contentment hovered silently.

A man strolled past with an empty water-container and stopped at the stand-tap to chat with Tom Douglas. Someone else was tipping his rubbish into a bin, discreetly concealed by a low wall. They ambled back together. The wife was hanging out a small washing on an improvised clothesline behind the caravan. Another, unhurried, was bringing a washing in. Quiet pleasure was in the simplest chore.

It was Maisie who eventually broke the silence.

"Clearly, a family man's holiday," she commented. "I don't think we'll beat superannuation here, Alison."

A late summer twilight was creeping over the caravan enclosure by the time the two friends returned from a quiet stroll up the lane beyond the site and back again. Lights appeared at the windows and the gay pattern of curtains spoke of cosiness within. Alison's own little van loomed up between two larger ones, its few cubic feet offering all the security that was needed.

She struck a match and the caravan was illumined by the light from the gas mantle. Maisie drew the curtains and Alison made them secure with little coloured clothes-pins.

"For sweet modesty's sake," she laughed. "Now, what price bed!"

A veritable vortex of activity followed. From the touch-line an astonished Maisie watched the rapid transformation of the living room into a sleeping apartment. There was a whirl of blankets, sleeping bags, pillows and night attire as they were dragged resisting from the hideaway beneath the upholstered cushions of the double bed. A flailing of arms followed as one half was transformed to the long window seat which suddenly emerged as a neatly made-up single bed. Another struggle and, hey presto, the second bed appeared. Once more order reigned.

Alison collapsed on the single bed.

"If you're not ready for bed before you get the beds made up," she gasped, "you're certainly ready afterwards."

They undressed and Maisie slipped into her sleeping bag. Viewed from a recumbent position, the small caravan presented a much more spacious aspect. It was now a roomy sleeping apartment.

Silence reigned. Somewhere a baby was crying.

There were a few conversational exchanges and then they settled for slumber.

"Good night, Alison," said Maisie.

"Good night, Maisie," said Alison. "Sleep well."

***

A new day dawned.

The sun was high in the heavens as they approached the summit of Ben Riach. Both wore slacks, shirt and boots and carried a rucksack. Alison sported a stout chestnut staff, her thumb inserted in the fork at the top end.

"To be a pilgrim!" she had chanted as they set out, the well-known hymn coming readily to mind.

"But without the bunion it's to be hoped!" punned the irrepressible Maisie. Alison chuckled appreciatively.

They were practised walkers and had readily surmounted the steep lower slopes, tramping unhesitatingly over stony tracks, crunching down jagged stones which yielded to the solid pressure of their Vibram-soled boots. On such an ascent Maisie appeared inexhaustible, her long legs bearing her tirelessly upwards. Alison was slower but she was dogged and had greater staying power than her friend, whose energy ultimately flagged more quickly.

The heather on the mountain side had reached its full purple glory. In the glen below, a stream wound sinuously round the lower slopes, fed by a number of cataracts which bounded laughing from a loch near the summit. The caravan site receded as they climbed, the white vans on the sward looking like a tiny washing put out to bleach on the green. There was not a single cloud on the horizon and the day was warm as only August days can be.

Alison stopped to rest on a flat rock which jutted out from the profusion of heather. She eased the straps of her haversack.

"On a day like this I want to live forever," she said simply.

Maisie laughed as she stretched out on the ground. She had been on holiday with Alison before and recognised the nostalgic tone.

"I don't want eternity," she replied cheerfully, "except 'to rest forever' as the hymn says. Life's hectic enough but I think I can face it if I know it *won't* go on forever. When the moment comes, just give me a celestial sleeping-bag and let me rest peacefully on a cloud."

She joined her hands prayerfully.

"You're a heretic." Alison laughed. "But actually, you look rather like a recumbent crusader lying there with your hands clasped. No, Maisie, the holiday mood is well and truly on me. In less than twenty-four hours after our arrival, I'm thoroughly unsettled and I love it."

A few moments later, they trudged on till they reached the loch set surprisingly in a hollow beneath the summit. The water was still and blue. At intervals round it a number of fishermen were to be seen silently absorbed in their pastime. Retracing their footsteps, the friends settled for lunch on the banks of a burn which descended the hillside in a series of cascades. In midstream two large boulders opposed their sleek sides to its onrush. Maisie straddled one and Alison perched on the other. It was a simple meal—cheese, apples and some chocolate biscuits, washed down by a draught of clear water which splashed into their cups as they stooped godlike to fill them from the burn.

The mood of the moment was one of supreme content. For Alison, the shared experience of enjoyment was one which she consciously valued, setting as it did an effective seal on the friendship. Maisie was one of many friends with whom she shared her recreational activities.

But there were others on whose friendship she set great store and whose qualities appealed to her for different reasons—Connie, who more readily shared her wilder flights of fancy; Laura who, like herself, had had a broken engagement but seemed to have weathered the storm rather more successfully; Kathleen, whom she had known since childhood; Jill, the patient listener, who could have such a soothing effect on her when irritated feelings required release.

Her withdrawal in recent years from the society of young men had meant a consequently greater involvement in relationships with her own sex. Though solidly based, these relationships, however, had not been unaffected by an underlying fear of rejection and this fear led her to spread her friendships widely. They were all best friends. Never again would she expose herself to over-involvement with any one person, man or woman. At thirty, her own peculiar need for defences found acceptance in a society whose social norms released her from the younger woman's self-respecting necessity of having a man on call.

Maisie's was an outgoing personality, strong and exuberant, but with a dormant sensitivity which provided the link between them. Romance had not featured so largely for her as for Alison, and there was a resultant area of unsatisfied longing in her life with which she had, nevertheless, come to terms in a reasonably satisfactory fashion.

It was still only early afternoon when they reached the summit along whose ridge was a grey outcrop of rock, which thrust itself into the air in a series of jagged peaks, hard and solid as the mountain itself. At one end of the ridge, the rock was replaced by an expanse of heather on which, close to each other but irregularly spaced, were a number of large boulders which presented something of the appearance of a druids' circle. One particularly massive group seemed to have fallen together in such a way as to leave a tunnelled aperture in the middle, extending to about five feet in length.

The friends approached it with interest.

"This must be Deirdre's Crag," exclaimed Maisie. "I'm sure the guide book said something about it."

She doffed her haversack and withdrew a limp-looking booklet which appeared to have nestled rather too closely to the chocolate biscuits.

She read: "…The aperture among the large stones at the north end of the ridge is known as Deirdre's Crag. Legend has it that if a single woman crawls through this aperture, she will be married within a three."

She replaced the booklet and grinned at her friend.

"Three months or three years, Alison, this is too good to miss," she said. "Matrimony, here I come!"

She pulled herself up on to the upper edge of the tunnel and peered through at Alison.

"A foot by eighteen inches or so," she mused. "I'll need to lose some weight."

Alison laughed.

"That's not the only problem," she replied. "I imagine the fates will be pretty particular about whether you go through headfirst or feet first, on your back or on your tummy."

Maisie's boots were already halfway through. She had chosen a supine position. Her head and shoulders still protruded from the other end and a characteristic gale of merriment shook her.

"Or whether you go from A to B or from B to A," she gasped. "I don't think the book said."

Alison too was convulsed.

"Well, on my reckoning that makes eight shots," she said when she had recovered her breath. "If you're not married by this time three years hence, Maisie, you'll have to try the other seven. Or will you do the lot now?"

Maisie's head eventually followed her legs and body through the aperture.

"Phew! No, I think that will do for the moment," she said. "I nearly got jammed halfway."

Alison approached the tunnel from the other side. To crawl through from this end meant a slight upward gradient and she chose to go through head first.

To have watched the ridged soles of Maisie's boots kicking a furious vertical passage through the gap had been uproarious. To find herself in a like position induced such hilarity that for minutes she could do nothing but lie flat in the stony passageway and laugh and laugh and laugh. Watching the curly head pillowed on the floor and listening to the helpless gurgles, Maisie collapsed weakly on the heather and, thus separated, the friends surrendered themselves wholly to uninhibited laughter.

The stones maintained a friendly silence. They had seen it all before. The sun smiled benevolently. A little breeze wafted approval. The heather stirred in quiet appreciation.

There was no question of the seven alternatives for either but later, as they swilled down coffee, they did speculate light-heartedly on whether, in the event of continued spinsterhood, these should be considered three summers thence in a single desperate bid, or whether a triennial effort should be the maximum permitted until they were—how old?

And then they took the downward way, varying the route slightly. They were tired but there was a sense of achievement. They had earned their evening meal. It had been a wonderful day.

Chapter VIII
The Second Caravan

Mr. Purdie strolled back to the caravan trundling his water-container behind him. The journey had been warm and consequently tiring. It was Saturday and the whole of Glasgow had seemed bent on making its escape from the city and on pushing competitively northwards. Congestion on the exit roads was heavy and there was an almost continual stream of traffic on the dual carriageway. The usual complement of visitors from the south mingled with the Scottish traffic. As many trailers bearing boat or camping equipment were to be seen as caravans. Some cars with caravans in the rear also carried boats on the roof. The car without an attachment presented a sober appearance, Mr. Purdie decided. People believed in working hard at their pleasures these days.

He had bought his caravan two years after his wife's death and consequently this was his third season on the road. He had done it to please Jane but had derived considerable pleasure from it himself. Elspeth, he knew, would never have agreed. She would have rebelled against holiday housekeeping, rendered difficult in the confined space. She would have disliked the caravan's sanitation arrangements only a little less than she would have disliked the communal toilets. Like many another housewife, she wanted a holiday to be more than a change of sink. She had needed it, Heaven knows, with her difficult pregnancies and subsequent depressions, and he had never grudged it to her. The enforced sociability of the family hotel, however, was a feature of the holiday which he had left behind without regret. Elspeth was no more gregarious than he himself and depended largely on him to make the convivial response. The dreaded last day when he had apprehensively asked for the bill was also something of the past.

No, the caravan had successfully solved both these problems. It combined the security of familiarity with the novelty of mobility.

From his moment of entry to a site, George's critical antennae were in action in exploratory assessment of its social tone. The transistor, the loud voice, the litter lout, the unsupervised child all irritated him inexpressibly. The advertisement of the small site with resident proprietor had attracted him as suggesting a degree of supervision, and his meeting with Tom Douglas confirmed this impression. The stroll to the stand-tap was therefore much more than a mere acquisition of water. It was his first venture forth on foot within the camp of the stranger, and he would return to Jane with news of the reconnoitre.

"They're nice people here, Jane," he would say. "Like ourselves."

And having set the seal of his approval on the site, Mr. Purdie was able to relax.

Jane would meanwhile busy herself about the caravan with a housewifely concern which was peculiarly lacking at home. She insisted on a supply of tablecloths and had embroidered one with lazy-daisy stitch during the winter especially for this holiday. Even her favourite dish-towels were included. The care with which she had spring-cleaned the van would have shamed even the excellent

Mrs. McSporran. There had been such a wiping of windows and scrubbing of floor, such a washing of crockery and cutlery, such a polishing and a shaking-up and restocking as had never been. True, some of the pristine glory had departed after the Easter holiday, but the continuing concern was ever-present.

Now she would get the meal ready for Daddy who was tired after driving all the way from Glasgow and who was now strolling round the site exchanging greetings with caravanners already settled. There was the gammon, lettuce, tomatoes and cucumber which would still be cool in the insulation bag. She arranged this neatly on plates and made some tea. Daddy liked potato salad and she opened a tin. There was tinned fruit and cream to follow. She surveyed the neatly set table with satisfaction.

Now, where was he? Oh, dear, he was talking again, first to the gentleman next door and now to two hikers with haversacks on their backs. It was always like this when she went anywhere with him. She only had to blink and he disappeared, or he had literally bumped into someone whose brother's friend's uncle knew a man who was related to a boyhood friend of his, and there was a subsequent need to exchange life histories.

Jane sat down and looked out at the cows who were making their way in stately procession down the slope of an adjoining field, following the matriarchal figure in the lead with unquestioning fidelity. It was really too bad and the tea would be cold. Who were these hikers anyway? Jane peeped out again through the opposite window. They were facing away from Jane—but wait! Jane's heart gave a leap, an exercise to which it had been unaccustomed for thirty-four days. The hikers were withdrawing from Mr. Purdie and making for a caravan which stood obliquely opposite the Purdies'. Suddenly, Jane's caravan seemed to become too small to contain the great uprush of emotion with which she was possessed, and she wanted to take off through the roof like a rocket on its way to Venus.

Miss Chalmers!

She jumped from the caravan as the only practical alternative, partly to share the discovery with her father, partly also in the hope that Miss Chalmers and Miss McTurk, as she now recognised her companion, would turn around and see her. But they were now inside the caravan.

Once again, Mr. Purdie wore his familiar smile of suppressed glee as he entered the caravan.

"Well, Jane, have you got my tea ready?" he demanded, naughtily aware that silence would only intensify his daughter's excitement.

"Oh, Daddy, that was Miss Chalmers!" exclaimed Jane quite unnecessarily.

"*And* Miss McTurk," her father corrected her. "Delightful ladies. I'll just have a cup of tea."

"But, Daddy," cried the thrilled but exasperated Jane, "you've actually spoken to her!"

Even her father's homely features assumed a new interest as belonging to one on whom the Queen of Heaven's eyes had rested and for whose ears the Queen of Heaven's lips had framed some few soft words.

Mr. Purdie poured out the tea. Still the humorous pursing of the lips. He passed Jane the bread.

"Daddy! Is she really staying here?"

"Mmmh? Speaking?"

There was such an eager questioning in Jane's eyes that Mr. Purdie could no longer maintain his assumed indifference and he burst out into a glad laugh.

"Isn't it a coincidence!" he exclaimed. "Miss Chalmers and Miss McTurk arrived only last night and they're staying for a week. Mr. Douglas is a friend of Miss Chalmers' brother. They've been up that mountain over there today."

Jane looked at it enthralled. In her eyes, it had already assumed the glory of Mount Olympus.

"We're here for a fortnight," she murmured, a faraway look in her eyes. "That means we'll see them every day."

After a pause, "Did you say anything about me?"

Mr. Purdie did not admit to Jane that Miss Chalmers had in fact said hardly anything to himself. He had come upon her suddenly near the entry to the field and had not at first recognised her. With boots and haversack, the two women had looked so different from the average slothful caravanner that he had looked at them with interest and at that moment Miss Chalmers' eyes had met his. His mind had flown instantly to the moment of his last meeting with her, in dress and academic gown, neatly groomed, cool— too cool?—and poised for the flight which he ultimately could not prevent.

They had momentarily stared at each other without giving a sign of recognition. It was Mr. Purdie who spoke the first word of greeting.

"Good evening, Miss Chalmers," he had said, raising his cap.

Quickly recovering her composure, Miss Chalmers had returned the greeting and hastily introduced Miss McTurk who responded with ready cordiality. The brief conversation which followed was for the most part between Miss McTurk and himself. He did not quite know what happened. He put a question to Miss Chalmers but it was Miss McTurk who answered and from there conversation developed between them. He had an impression on taking his leave that Miss Chalmers was badly discomfited, but it did nothing to dampen his own elation.

**

In the other caravan, the friends dropped thankfully to their seats and Alison pushed open a window, their haversacks and boots stood outside.

Maisie pulled a face.

"We'll have to behave," she said wryly. "No lounging outside the van in our bikinis."

Alison smiled but said nothing.

"He seemed very friendly," went on Maisie. "You've met him before?"

Alison nodded casually.

"Once or twice, at school functions."

A pause.

"Well, I could do with a shower," said Maisie. "Are you coming?"

**

The site wore its usual morning mantle of stillness. The birds in the nearby trees proclaimed that dawn had broken. Imperceptibly, the sun mounted the further side of Ben Riach, giving promise of long sunlit hours ahead. The drawn-to curtains of fifteen gleaming caravans bore witness to the slumber which held the occupants in thrall. From fifty-five souls arose a great sleep while the beauty of the morning unfolded.

A closer inspection would have revealed that only fifty-four souls slept. The fifty-fifth lay wakeful. The previous night a healthy sleep had quickly overwhelmed

Alison following the exertions of the day, but at five she was wide awake, her mind active.

First and foremost, last but far from least, George Purdie came between Alison and her dreams. It would perhaps be truer to say that George Purdie had been her dream. There had been no sequence of events in this dream. No happenings, nothing either pleasant or unpleasant. Just a face, George Purdie's, which, like yesterday's sun, shone and shone and shone. It had been there before she dropped off; it was there throughout her sleep, and ultimately became so real that it broke right through her sleep and woke her up.

He was not good-looking but there was a square strength about him that had arrested her attention. There was a squareness in his jaw and a squareness in his shoulders and a squareness in his stride. There was a squareness in the very cap he wore. His voice was deep and had a certain resonance, almost as though it were proceeding from the depths of a high-vaulted cavern. But George Purdie was no caveman. His every word and gesture expressed propriety. He was a model of middle-class respectability. But did not every man have something of the caveman in his make-up, George Purdie included? Was it possible that he too was seeking his cavewoman?

Whether he had sought others after the death of Jane's mother, Alison did not know, but of one thing she was certain. He was certainly seeking a mate now and had shown her this in a dozen different ways.

At their first meeting in the school hall he had, of course, appeared as no more than the concerned father, unsure of himself in unfamiliar surroundings. But he had been completely at ease at the school sports, first when they had had ice-cream together and later when he had helped her carry the container. They had chatted about this and that and Alison had found him a pleasing companion. The subject matter was of little importance— the sports, school—but words had flitted to and fro between them, creating an illusion of triviality while communication at a deeper level was taking place. She was vaguely aware that it had been a long time since she had spoken face to face with a man. Almost unconsciously, she had stretched out to grasp what had been almost as unconsciously offered. By the end of the afternoon, she knew that it had happened. It was as though she had mounted a chariot and galloped off she knew not where, not even caring, because someone else held the reins and she was content to leave the planning of the course to him.

That afternoon her experience had been extended by the addition of another dimension, to which she had been for long a stranger. She remembered that she was a woman.

And with this realisation came memories of Alastair and Hector and heartbreak. To be a woman was to be vulnerable and to be vulnerable was to know the meaning of heartbreak, and twice had been twice too often. Let love in at the door and common-sense flew out at the window. Before it overwhelmed her like a narcotic she must resist, and she had feebly endeavoured to refuse George Purdie's offer of help with the ice-cream container.

She had eluded him at the school concert, she supposed, because she was behind the scenes. It was too much to expect the same on Prize Day. He had not forced his attention on her. The greeting had been that of parent to teacher, and once again these deceptive light-hearted words had taken over. It all seemed so harmless. Was she deceiving herself that *he* was attracted? Was she deceiving herself that *she* was attracted? But the eager look in his eyes when they shook hands and his reluctance to let her hand go confirmed the reality of the situation.

Holidays came with more than the usual relief and she threw herself hastily into her preparations for the cruise, in which older girls and staff were participating and which was scheduled for departure only three days later. It had been a successful excursion and by the end of July, Alison had managed to forget what she regarded as an emotional lapse, even to smile at the memory of her apprehension.

But since last night when she had encountered Mr. Purdie so unexpectedly, she knew that she was trapped. With the fatalism which had corroded her philosophy of life in recent years, she accepted the inevitability of the situation, though her instinct was for immediate flight.

She glanced over at Maisie whose peaceful breathing indicated a tranquillity strangely at variance with her own troubled emotions. From a recumbent position, the caravan always looked unusually spacious. She looked up at the arched ceiling, the cupboard which she had forgotten to slide shut, the tray on which stood the teacup from which Maisie had insisted on drinking before turning in, despite the possibility of a toilet-trot during the night. She had so looked forward to this, her first real holiday in the caravan as opposed to weekend jaunts, and now a new element threatened.

Out of the depths of a badly wounded personality had emerged a woman who, at one level, had lost faith in herself. In a supremely important area of her life, she had twice been relegated to a position of second best—second to the woman who had come to monopolise Alastair, second to the wife from whom Hector would not break— and subconsciously, she had come to regard herself as someone who could be taken seriously only up to a certain point. Her success in other areas of life had never quite compensated for this, and she shrank from the possibility of a repetition of the particular brand of experience which she had come to believe had been decreed for her.

She sighed involuntarily. Reliable as Mr. Purdie might seem, Alison could foresee nothing in the developing situation but that of the doomed craft being drawn ever nearer to destruction by a masculine Lorelei. Impossible to leave Tom Douglas' caravan site within forty-eight hours when they had booked for a week. Peter would hear of it and would feel she had let his friend and himself down. Maisie would be at a loss regarding the change of plan and—good friend that she was—might just not understand her own urgent need for departure. Besides, Maisie had already told Mr. Purdie they were here for a week, and Mr. Purdie had doubtless told Jane and Jane would tell… Again she sighed. The situation would be laughable if it were not causing her such apprehension.

She looked at her watch. Six thirty a.m. They had agreed to rise around half past eight. On the one hand, she longed to leap out of bed and get the day started, any old way. It would end the dreadful tension of waiting. On the other hand, bed spelt security and she could have wished the hands of her watch to stay forever at six thirty a.m. on this quiet site with not a soul stirring.

***

As soon as Jane woke up, she cautiously lifted one corner of the curtain and peeped out. It had been so exciting to go to bed only a few yards away from Miss Chalmers. She had sent her a whispered goodnight and blown her a kiss through the partially open window. With morning, her first thoughts were for the caravan opposite, but the curtains were still shut and there was no sign of life. Above and beyond it loomed the mountain that Miss Chalmers and Miss McTurk had climbed. A poetic example of personification crossed Jane's mind.

"But, look, the morn, in russet mantle clad,

Walks o'er the dew of yon high eastward hill."

It was Miss Chalmers herself who had written this on the board during a lesson on figures of speech.

She mouthed the couplet, not wishing to disturb her father and also from a feeling of delicacy that it belonged specially to Miss Chalmers and herself. Moreover, it served as a nice little prologue to her own verses which she now silently repeated.

"Oh, gracious lady, fair and sweet,

I lay my heart down at your feet."

Her father still lay asleep, separated from her by a bright chintz curtain, which divided the caravan in two.

An hour later, washed and shaved, he took his usual stroll round the site. He too noticed that the curtains of the caravan on Pitch No.5 were still drawn-to.

Jane, having set the table and put the kettle on, crossed to the drain with the slop-pail which could not have had more than three or four pints in it from the previous night's washing-up, but she wanted an excuse for leaving the caravan.

"What are we doing today, Daddy?" she asked at breakfast.

"I think we should take it easy today, Jane," he replied, "at least for the morning."

Jane looked disappointed. She did not like taking it easy.

"But if we don't do anything, Miss Chalmers will think we're not very interesting," she replied, "and if we hang about, she might think we were watching her."

It was with small satisfaction that Mr. Purdie recognised an echo of the homily on restraint which he had delivered when Jane had wanted to follow Miss Chalmers' car after the concert.

"I think we should climb that mountain," suggested Jane, "and then we could tell Miss Chalmers that we've been up it too."

Mr. Purdie said nothing and Jane was unable to draw him further.

The curtains of the caravan at Pitch No.5 were now open, and Mr. Purdie had ascertained from a surreptitious look in that direction that the occupants were at breakfast.

The washing-up complete, father and daughter came into competition as to who should empty the slop-pail, into which the washing-up water had flowed through the pipe beneath the caravan. The pail had a capacity of three gallons and did not need emptying.

"It's all right, Daddy, I'll empty it," said Jane in what she hoped was a kindly tone. "You sit down and rest."

"No, Jane, I'll do it," replied Mr. Purdie with like concern. "I've always said it was too heavy for you."

"But there's hardly anything in it," objected Jane.

"Then, why do you want to empty it?" returned Mr. Purdie, grasping it firmly and sauntering casually to the drain.

Realising his own inconsistency and that his tone had been rather sharper than usual, he turned around as he went.

"Empty the rubbish pail, Jane," he called. "It's got all those tins from last night."

They usually shared chores but this morning Mr. Purdie would have preferred to empty the rubbish pail as well. He too wanted to be seen, but more than that he wanted to talk to Miss Chalmers and explore further a personality which he found exciting.

Breakfast in the other caravan still appeared to be in progress. Mr. Purdie was nonplussed. By this time on a Sunday, he was usually strolling to the nearest shop for his Sunday paper but he was loath to leave the site.

***

Alison and Maisie surveyed the crumbs on the breakfast plates.

"Father Purdie and Jane seem busy," remarked Maisie cheerfully.

The window by the table looked up to the Ben, but the window at the other end of the caravan gave on to the site.

"Mrs. Purdie's keeping well out of the way."

There was a pause before Alison answered.

"There isn't a Mrs. Purdie," she said.

Maisie looked surprised.

"I believe she died a few years ago."

Maisie said "Oh!" then added, "That's very sad. I'd forgotten. Does that mean there's just the two of them over there?"

Alison nodded. "I suppose so," she replied.

"Not much of a holiday for Mr. Purdie," commented Maisie, "or for Jane."

Another pause. Suddenly, Maisie laughed.

"Is it to be you or me?" she asked. "Remember Deirdre's Crag! I would say the fates directed Mr. Purdie's car to this site the moment you—or I—slid through!"

Alison made an effort to fit in with Maisie's mood.

"Well, what are we going to do about it?" she demanded, smiling in spite of herself.

Maisie knit her brows.

"Let's invite them over one evening," she suggested. "You can help Jane brush up her Shakespeare and I'll take Mr. Purdie for a walk. How'z'at for a midsummer night's dream?"

Again, Alison smiled a smile that was not quite her own.

"Seriously, though," went on Maisie, "it might be a good idea. Mr. Purdie seems a sensible man, he may be lonely and it could brighten up our lives!"

"Let's not be in too much of a hurry," countered Alison, rising as she spoke and gathering the crockery together. "We've got the rest of the week."

They did the washing-up together.

"I vote we take it easy today," said Maisie, replacing the cutlery in its box. "We made an energetic start yesterday. Let's have some Sabbath rest."

Alison did not reply immediately. Had circumstances been ordinary she would have been ready either to agree or to put forward her own point of view. But circumstances were not ordinary. She was acutely conscious of the caravan opposite, and whatever decision they came to today and other days would have to be viewed in relation to what she knew to be the total situation. She felt incapable of making a suggestion herself but was nervous about leaving the decision-making to Maisie.

Helplessly she said, "What do you suggest?"

"Well," said Maisie, "We could take the garden-loungers out of the boot and sit around until lunch-time, or…" Clearly, Maisie wanted to sit around.

Did Mr. Purdie? Alison yielded. "Yes, that would be nice," she agreed.

It was difficult to be enthusiastic about A or a hypothetical B when she was really grappling with alternatives C and D, neither of which seemed practicable. One part of her wanted to mount that delightful chariot again, so that she could again give herself up to the experience, at once relaxing and stimulating, of surrendering the reins to another. The other part of her was trying to conjure up the reality of the last few years— her many friends, her multiple interests, the security of independent living; and with memories of her uphill struggle to achieve this, she had an impulse to hurl herself into the car and make a headlong getaway.

And now, they were stretched out on the garden-loungers, as were many of their neighbours. Despite the heat, Mrs. Floss, as they still called her, had decided to wash the windows of her caravan. Mr. Floss was reading the Sunday paper with Candy lying at his side on the warm grass. The family on the other side had gone to church. Maisie, in shorts and sun-top, was soaking up the sun—Jane Purdie could report what she liked to her pals. Alison's appearance, in sleeveless blouse and light-weight slacks, was rather more conservative. A protective hat, a relic of childhood, was tilted rakishly on her forehead and she wore sunglasses.

She was trying to read, in the hope of channelling her thoughts in a neutral direction. But it was not easy. From the shelter of the panama hat and the sunglasses, she squinted up at the caravan on Pitch No.2. The occupants had gone, but not in their car. Perhaps they had set off while she and Maisie had been organising the garden-loungers. Had they gone for the stroll which they themselves had taken on the night of their arrival? If so, that would occupy them until lunch-time. Or had they gone to the village shop which was only a step away?

The words of her book stared back at her meaninglessly. She allowed her eyes to travel along the line, then from one line to another, then over to the next page, without absorbing any of it. Maisie, she knew, was in her element and was obviously unaware of the tumult of emotions that she was struggling against. She abandoned hope of the carefree, companionable holiday which the previous day had promised. She must play a part so as not to spoil the week for Maisie and in order to keep her own end up.

A shadow fell across the page and she looked up. It was Mr. Purdie and Jane. Both smiled eagerly down at her and she found herself smiling back. With the intrusion of reality, she felt her anxieties receding.

Mr. Purdie carried a Sunday paper and a large paper bag.

"Good morning, ladies," he greeted them. "It was so hot that I felt a service of ice-cream was called for. Would you care to join me?"

"How very kind of you, Mr. Purdie," exclaimed Alison, removing her hat and sunglasses. "It's just what we need."

The semi-recumbent Maisie echoed her acknowledgement and, having adjusted the angle of the garden-lounger, accepted the carton gratefully.

Mr. Purdie and Jane sat on the grass. For the moment, Alison appeared to have regained her composure.

"And how does caravan life suit you, Jane?" she asked.

This was Jane's first face-to-face encounter with Miss Chalmers since their arrival. The smile which she had looked for in vain at prize-giving had now been given. She could ask no more.

Alison was suddenly conscious of the tone she had used in addressing Jane. Once more she was the teacher and she figuratively grasped at the academic gown in which she saw a defence. As Jane's teacher she had met Mr. Purdie and as Jane's teacher she would conduct herself. A voice from within laughed mockingly.

The sun shone and the ice-cream slid down and the conversation was pleasantly informal. For three out of the four it was Sports Day, squared. It was Sports Day to the nth degree. Three out of the four knew a happiness akin to ecstasy. For the fourth, the pleasure was of a more sober order.

***

It was Wednesday. Three days had passed as only three days on holiday can when a change of location turns time upside down and makes an afternoon seem like a day and a day like three.

To Jane, it was as though she had stepped on to another planet. At school, she had thankfully pecked at the crumbs from the rich man's table as far as emotional satisfaction was concerned. She had gleaned the scattered smile loosed by the Ceres of the moment and, knowing nothing else, had felt it to be a most plenteous crop. But since their arrival in the Glen, a veritable horn of plenty had poured its contents into her lap. A third dimension had entered her life and she felt infinitely enriched.

There had been coincidence after coincidence. She and Daddy had gone to Loch Beg where there were boats for hire, and behold! Miss Chalmers and Miss McTurk had already arrived. They had followed a Nature Trail through Glen Malloch and had met them again. En route to Kilmadden Castle they had come on the two teachers struggling vainly to loosen the over-stiff nuts on a wheel which had suffered a puncture. How proud she had been when Daddy had applied his strong brown hands to the job and changed the wheel for them.

Either Daddy or she herself seemed continually to be meeting either Miss Chalmers or Miss McTurk at the stand-tap, or at the slop-drain, or at the bins. For herself she was almost as pleased when she met Miss McTurk as when she met Miss Chalmers, for Miss McTurk, unknown to herself, had donned a mantle of reflected glory.

There were smiles in plenty for her from both teachers. At one point, she was apprehensive lest she and Daddy should be in Miss Chalmers' way, but she experienced daily reassurance on that point.

At night, she sent an affectionate message through the fading light to Miss Chalmers. In the bright light of day, it was less easy but she contrived to lift a tiny corner of the curtain and to breathe a morning greeting through the open window.

She drew satisfaction from her observation that her father shared her enthusiasm for Miss Chalmers. They had been so close, father and daughter, over the years and Jane had identified with most of his attitudes. In this new and most important aspect of her life therefore, it was gratifying that they should once more be united.

It was perhaps not unnatural that she should regard herself as the senior partner in this venture. Had she not known Miss Chalmers much longer than he, and was it not through herself that her father had come to meet Miss Chalmers? Moreover, once school started she, alone of the two, would be in daily contact with the object of their joint admiration and would be able to report to him, as the less privileged partner, the events of the day, which would form the basis of the partnership's transactions.

It would have been difficult to say at what point a wind of change blew into the situation. Looking back, Jane knew that all was well on Wednesday morning, but by Thursday evening she was much less certain and by Friday the sun had vanished from her sky.

It was Wednesday at tea-time. Jane had returned home with her father from a day of varied activity—driving, walking, bathing and picnicking. They had eaten well and there was no need for an immediate meal. They sat within the caravan, relaxed and a little weary. Both, of course, were fully aware that the occupants of Pitch No.5 were in residence. The car was there. The door of the caravan was open and the haversacks were propped outside. The two teachers did not appear to be in the caravan because Jane from her oblique viewpoint could see one half of the interior through the open door and the other half through the window.

Suddenly, Miss Chalmers appeared from the direction of the toilet block, alone. She was carrying sponge-bag, towel and some articles of clothing from which she had just changed. She had acquired an attractive tan and looked very youthful in a light cotton dress which had replaced the daytime slacks.

Jane looked at her own dusty footwear, her well-worn jeans and unwashed hands. It had not occurred to her to have a shower. Mr. Purdie was conservative in his tastes and would as soon have flown to the moon as indulge in an orgy of cleansing by a method so different from the bath in which he liked to soak at home. In any case she would have wanted more privacy than was afforded by the plastic curtain in the double shower closet. Lovingly, she looked over at the neat figure whose attractions she felt she could not possibly emulate, and there was pain as well as pleasure in the beholding.

Miss Chalmers entered her caravan and re-emerged with a purse and a string bag. Jane would have liked nothing more than to take her place by Miss Chalmers' side and to walk with her to the village and back, but she knew she must behave. Accordingly, she did not move but followed with her eyes.

She experienced a mild shock therefore when, without a word, her father rose abruptly and left the van, striding after the retreating form. Had he said that he wanted something from the shop she would have immediately gone along with him, relying on his sense of propriety as to the wisdom of the proposed link-up. But the suddenness of the action took her by surprise, as did the implied wish to exclude her. The inhibition which restrained her was as strong as the impulse to follow, and she watched her father make up on Miss Chalmers who seemed to hesitate a moment before continuing on her way in his company. She watched as they skirted Mr. Douglas' wall and rounded the patch of woodland which screened the site from the main road to the village.

In due course, Miss McTurk appeared from the toilet block, also bearing a sponge-bag, towel and clothing, and sauntered casually over to the caravan, unaware that Jane's eyes were upon her.

There was something reassuring about the careless ease with which Miss McTurk crossed the sward but Jane was not reassured. She wanted to run over to report the disturbing news, but the need to contain her feelings was dominant and she was aware, as though for the first time, that her father and Miss Chalmers had something to share in which she could not possibly participate and the thought was disquieting. As she grappled anxiously with the half-formed questions in her mind, she knew too that the surprise element in the situation was to some extent spurious. She had wanted a link-up between these two vital persons, she had rejoiced at the widely spaced but apparently divinely decreed encounters. It was supremely natural that her father should want to be alone with the object of their mutual admiration, just as she would have liked to be. He would not have grudged her the pleasure so why should she grudge it to him?

But she did.

She sat motionless in the caravan, the scene of Saturday evening's ecstasy when she had first seen Miss Chalmers. There was a world of difference in the respective levels recorded on her emotional barometer by the two events, and her emotions could not catch up with the understanding which told her that the one was as irrational as the other.

Twenty minutes passed. Half an hour. She saw Miss McTurk at the door of the caravan looking towards the lane which passed Mr. Douglas' cottage and skirted the little wood. Jane wondered if she too would feel neglected if she were to discover that her friend was not alone. No, not neglected. That was not how she would have described her unpleasant agitation. It was like—yes, she had experienced something similar on Prize Day when Miss Chalmers had hurried away so suddenly. The memory of the succeeding weeks of unhappiness returned to her, and for the first time she found herself focussing attention on her father's uncharacteristic silence during that period, a factor which had hitherto been only on the periphery of her consciousness.

It all fell into line with a rather frightening clarity and her own awakened anxiety compelled her to wrest a reassuring explanation from the two occurrences which had brought her within the fringe of the unknown.

Yes, that was it. Daddy had been upset too when Miss Chalmers had hurried away on Prize Day. Perhaps he thought he had offended her and now he was taking the opportunity of asking her about this in private. A smile had been sufficient to compensate herself for the prior omission, but grown-ups sometimes took things more seriously. He had not up until now had the chance to speak to Miss Chalmers alone, and he had decided to snatch this opportunity while Miss McTurk was elsewhere.

She found a measure of satisfaction in the rationalisation which enabled her to emerge from her immobility. She rose and at that moment she caught sight of her father and Miss Chalmers returning. Yes, of course, everything was all right.

Mr. Purdie was not really aware of the scrutiny which he had to undergo as Jane anxiously tried to extract from his expression signs of reassurance or anxiety. It was as though nothing had happened. He made no comment about his absence and Jane asked no question. Without knowing why, she knew that she was afraid of the answer.

Chapter IX
Water-Skiing

"How do you fancy water-skiing?" asked Mr. Purdie the following morning.

Jane's face lit up. She had seen water-skiing on television and it looked exciting.

She indicated eager interest.

"Mr. Douglas has a friend with a couple of speed-boats and some skis on Loch Darroch," said Mr, Purdie. "It might be fun to watch."

Jane needed no encouragement. She seldom lacked energy and today she felt a particular need for diversion.

The tenants of Pitch No.5 were still breakfasting when father and daughter set off, neither making a comment.

Jane almost sighed with relief as the car turned from the dusty lane on to the main road and set off in the direction of Loch Darroch about twenty miles away. There was a whole world outside the caravan site. Today was a new day, the sun was shining again and Daddy's idea was a good one. She started to chatter as usual as they drove along and Mr. Purdie made his usual responses.

Loch Darroch was surrounded on three sides by hills, from one of which Mr. Purdie made his approach after a climb of several miles on an undulating road. A few yards from the roadside, on its flatter stretches, a burn had danced towards them and cascaded in a number of little waterfalls to a series of lower levels. Heather-clad slopes rose on either side. Little knots of people were already assembling for the day in intermittent grassy clearings on either side of the road, complete with gaily-coloured folding chairs and picnic tables. Children were racing little twig boats on the swiftly flowing burn. Others mounted the nearer hillocks in make-believe mountaineering. Some figures were already advancing along the track which led invitingly over the hills and far away.

Further on there was a fleeting glimpse, far below the level of the road, of a loch cradled among the fir-covered slopes. Even as Jane cried out at its beauty it was gone, and Mr. Purdie rounded another bend.

They first caught sight of Loch Darroch as they descended from the highest point of the road, blue as the sky above and without a ripple to disturb the surface. The foliage of the trees on the lower slopes of the road tended to obscure the view as they approached water-level, but as they circled the end of the loch, the view opened out and they were able to see clearly.

Half a mile or so along the other side stood a little hut on the shore, and a few yards away a jetty projected out into the water. A speedboat lay alongside it. Further out a second speedboat was circling round in a wide arc. Some yards behind followed the figure of a man on skis, skimming like a swallow along the surface of the water. As the speedboat continued its wide sweep, the figure swung out from the wake to trace an even wider arc. The boatman made a hand signal and changed direction. The skier's response was to cut across the wake and to swing out to the other side. Boat and skier repeated the action and then set off down the loch, crossing and re-crossing the wake alternately.

"Gosh, that looks exciting," said Jane.

Presently, the first boat roared into action and another skier offered himself up to the combined delights of water, sunshine and speed. Unlike the first skier, he had one ski only, his speed was greater, and as he swung out from one side of the wake to the other his body swerved, like that of a speedway cyclist, until his shoulder almost touched the water. A plume of spray arose like a protective screen, vanishing as he emerged in continued flight.

Father and daughter were intrigued, and when a number of other motorists pulled up, they decided to watch from a closer viewpoint.

The shore was sandy on either side of the jetty, and as the morning advanced numbers of holiday-makers arrived, attracted by advertising in local hotels and in the nearby holiday town of West Morton. Those who elected to ski were mostly young men and children but occasionally a girl would join in. Many appeared practised skiers and provided expert entertainment for those who had come solely to view. No less entertaining, but of a different order, was the performance of those who were skiing for the first time and who had to endure a number of spills in their attempted take-off. The crowd was in holiday mood and, though ready to laugh at the belly-flops, quickly showed themselves in sympathy with beginners, to whom they afforded a friendly handclap with every improved attempt.

"Do you want to try?" asked Mr. Purdie when they had been watching for some time.

Jane nodded eagerly. There was a challenge in this new sport which made a strong appeal.

Having changed into her costume and been invested with a life jacket, she took her place in a small queue of three. There were two instructors, an elderly man with beard and moustache who sported a seaman's cap, and a young fellow in shorts.

At last, it was Jane's turn and Bob, the older man, was to take her out. She had already listened carefully to the instructions given to the others, "Arms straight, keep the points of your skis above water level, let the boat pull you up," and decided it was as easy as the experts made it, despite the evidence to the contrary from fellow beginners.

But when she mounted the jetty carrying the brightly coloured skis, she knew sudden panic. It seemed so like the scaffold. She was even carrying the instruments of her execution. Mary Queen of Scots, Anne Boleyn and Charles I swam horrifyingly into her mind, and the friendly crowds suddenly became a mob who had gathered to see her die. She wanted to turn back, but her bare feet padded mechanically along to the end where Bob was awaiting her in his boat, gathering in the rope and towbar which still trailed in the water where it had been dropped at the conclusion of the previous run.

Bob gave her an encouraging smile and, having laid the coiled-up rope on the rear deck, he clambered out to help her fit on her skis.

Jane was afraid but she was even more afraid of the indignity of retreat and submitted to Bob's assistance, while the familiar words of instruction passed right over her head.

Now she was endeavouring to take her seat on the end of the jetty, an almost impossible task with her feet elongated at both ends by the skis. She leaned back ungracefully, her feet in the air, but this was the move necessary to get her skis over the side. She felt the swirl of the water round her ankles. Bob's boat was already several feet from the jetty. From a standing position, he threw her the towbar. For a wonder, she caught it.

It was more like the scaffold than ever, she quaked. No, the gallows. In another minute, the boat would roar into life, the rope would become taut and, clinging to the towbar, she would be dragged off the end of the jetty. Could anything be more like the long drop!

Helplessly, she turned round to see if her father were watching. Yes, he was there and he waved. But someone else was there too, two people. Miss Chalmers and Miss McTurk, and both waved to her.

Mechanically, she returned the wave but the greeting from the three observers on the shore failed to generate the elation which two days previously would have been certain. The distress of the previous evening again assailed her, replacing her fear of take-off with something infinitely less manageable. Behind her was the Scylla of nameless disquiet. In front was the Charybdis of sheer naked fear. Half-consciously and with only limited understanding, she opted for the latter as providing a form of shock treatment.

"Get the rope between your skis," shouted Bob. "Arms straight! Lean back! Let the boat pull you up."

The slack on the deck gradually paid out as the boat chugged away from the jetty. Jane grasped the towbar as though her very life depended on it. Another coil dropped off the end of the boat and another and another.

"Ready to go!" shouted Bob and the engine roared.

Flop!

Sixty seconds later, Jane crawled out of the water, ignominiously aware that Miss Chalmers had witnessed her failure but with some of the distress dispelled. The challenge of take-off re-asserted itself.

Again, she took up her position on the jetty and Bob threw her the towbar.

"Get yourself right on the end of the jetty," he advised. "Lean well back and let the boat pull you up."

Again, the surge of fear and the roar of take-off. Again, the dunking and again the brisk intrusion of reality as the mellow waters of the loch closed momentarily and harmlessly over her head.

She tried again and yet again. She fell forward on her face and backwards on her back and to the left and to the right. Once, when she thought she had managed it, the skis went splay in front of her. There was loch water in her eyes and in her ears and she felt as though a good half of the loch was in her tummy. But she found satisfaction in the effort. She was struggling for more than the mastery of a new technique. Unconsciously, she equated the achievement of balance on the skis with the symbolic balance required in the new and uncertain course her life had taken.

"Hard lines," grinned Bob. "You'll get it next time. It's just like learning to ride a bicycle."

A bicycle! His words struck a deep chord. She had a sudden mental picture of her first bicycle and of her father holding her steady, and of the hard, white road stretching ahead of her. If only he could hold her steady now!

She dripped her way off the jetty and over to where Mr. Purdie and the two teachers were standing.

"Very well tried," said her father. Jane could not help smiling. His commendation meant a great deal.

"Try a deep water start next time," advised Miss Chalmers. "I'll hold you."

Jane knew a glow of happiness. Everything was all right again. Daddy was pleased with her. Miss Chalmers was going to help her. Last night was last night but today was today. "Are you going to try, Daddy?" she asked.

Mr. Purdie shook his head.

"I'll maybe have a swim later, Jane," he said, "but I think I'd rather watch other folks on skis than try myself."

Miss Chalmers and Miss McTurk had meanwhile retreated into the hut to don costumes and wet suits.

"A wet suit gives added buoyancy and protection if you take a fall further out," Miss McTurk had explained.

Jane had seen skiers wearing these black wet suits on the TV screen. It was with a measure of relief that she beheld Miss Chalmers and Miss McTurk thus decently attired. She would have experienced intense embarrassment had she seen her heroine in the semi-nudity of a bathing suit, especially in the knowledge of her father's interest.

The two ladies had obviously skied before and had come equipped. It was in fact their third call at the loch this week.

Whoosh! Miss Chalmers was away, skiing behind Bob as she herself had done, while Miss McTurk awaited young Johnnie's return.

Jane noticed that a few yards from the jetty Miss Chalmers deftly stepped out of the right ski, and transferred her foot to a position on the remaining ski, just behind her left foot. So this was how the Monoski position was achieved. Jane watched fascinated as Miss Chalmers swung out wide of the wake, to cross it and re-cross it with never a spill, taking its bump easily and lightly, pulling hard at the point of furthest extension before soaring again to the opposite extremity. Jane's heart filled with adoration. Was there anything Miss Chalmers could not do!

Miss McTurk was next, skiing behind Johnnie, and she appeared equally skilled, circling first on two skis within an easy radius of the jetty and shedding one as she re-passed it.

One ski! And she, Jane, could not manage two, which was easier.

Jane put her name down for another turn. There were beginners and improvers as well as experts on Bob's list, and she hoped to graduate from her present undistinguished grade.

And now Bob was thundering back to the jetty with Miss Chalmers on his tail. With expert timing, she released her hold of the towbar so that the impetus from the boat flagged just as she drew level with the jetty. Neatly, she took her seat on the end of it like a seabird coming to rest.

"Thanks, Bob," she called and leaned down to detach the ski.

Miss Chalmers did indeed peel off her wet suit when she had rejoined Jane and Mr. Purdie. Being wet, it clung tightly to both arms and her effort was unavailing.

"Jane, will you give me a hand?" she asked, but it was Mr. Purdie who reached her first. Jane averted her gaze. His assistance in the disrobing act suggested an intimacy which shocked her. She was unable to recognise her father and teacher in those two laughing, carefree holiday-makers between whom something more than friendship had inexplicably developed.

Soon, it was Jane's turn again. True to her word, Miss Chalmers came down to the water with her and together they waded in. Jane's wading was slow because of the ski attachment. "Big banana feet" were the words which sang in her ears, before the water lapped over her ankles covering them up. She reached waist level and Bob threw her the towbar.

"Lean back," ordered Miss Chalmers. Jane obeyed as though in a dream and felt Miss Chalmers' hands in her oxters. The skis came up and, as instructed, Jane flicked the rope between them and straightened her arms. Bob chugged slowly out and the rope arose dripping from the water, till it was taut between them. Jane sat back in the water, comfortably aware of Miss Chalmers' support but bewildered by her sudden change of role. Was it possible that such friendly concern could emanate from the same person, who had flaunted herself so shamelessly only a few minutes since?

"Ready to go!" shouted Bob.

The engine roared. Jane pressed hard with her feet and this time succeeded in keeping her skis parallel. Still in the crouching position of take-off, she skied out into the loch, oblivious of everything except success. She had made it!

The sun glowed and the breeze of her own making blew refreshingly on her face and arms. Bob was signing to her to rise to her feet and though reluctant to abandon her hard-won security, she accepted the challenge and found it easier than she had expected. Like Mananan's daughter, she rose from the loch. Over his shoulder Bob grinned his pleasure. Breathlessly, she smiled back.

The water was like glass. Only in the wake was there a degree of turbulence and she could not as yet risk crossing over the bump on its edge, even to reach the tantalising stillness beyond. She looked at her sunburnt hands and at the towbar which they clasped so desperately. She looked down at her feet encased in the black rubber fitting, and at her own brown legs and at the gay red skis bumping gently along the wake of the speed-boat. The spray washed her ankles.

She was triumphantly aware of the blueness of the loch and the blueness of the sky and of the mingled green and purple of the hills. She was intoxicated with the motion and sufficiently uncertain of the new technique to feel a keen edge to her enjoyment. For the moment she was, in very truth, Queen of the Loch!

She had not been aware of the plaudits of the crowd on the beach who had witnessed her eventual success, but she happily accepted the congratulations of the three who awaited her on her return.

"Well done," said her father.

"Did you enjoy it?" asked Miss Chalmers.

"Monoski next time," said Miss McTurk.

Jane's barometer of happiness recorded a new all-time high. With smiles all round, success on the skis, her father's approval and the sun in the sky, how could it be otherwise!

Miss Chalmers and Miss McTurk each had another turn on the skis and then a picnic was shared. Oh, it was wonderful!

This was the first time they had all shared an outing. Whatever would Madge and Fiona say when she told them whom she had met on holiday!

"Who feels like ice-cream?" asked Miss Chalmers when they had finished eating.

"I wish I *did* feel like ice-cream," replied the jocular Miss McTurk, "Just at the moment I feel more like a blob of grease."

"Is there any to be had around?" asked Mr. Purdie.

"Yes, there's a mobile van in the car park," replied Miss Chalmers. "At least there was when we were here the other day."

"Let me get you some," said Mr. Purdie, rising to his feet.

"No, no," countered Miss Chalmers, also rising. "Please, Mr. Purdie, it's my turn. I must insist."

She slipped a cotton skirt over her costume. Miss McTurk continued to sprawl lazily on the sun-lounger. Sun, sun, sun, that was all she asked.

Jane looked up eagerly. Perhaps she could run the errand for them but it seemed that Daddy had other ideas.

"Let me help you carry it then," he said to Miss Chalmers. "*I* must insist."

And they were away.

Jane glanced over at the recumbent Miss McTurk, looking now so different from the active hockey player of the spring. She looked along the leafy path leading up to the road along, which her father and Miss Chalmers had vanished.

Prize Day! Last night! And now again. The tottering security of a Macbeth might well have wrung from her the bitter statement of fact, 'Then comes my fit again.' But they had only done 'A Midsummer Night's Dream' so far.

Once again, she found herself a prey to that unpleasant agitation. It was all Daddy's fault. Could he not have been satisfied with his walk to the village last night? He was surely now just causing annoyance to Miss Chalmers who wanted to be generous. Or... An appalling thought struck Jane. Had Miss Chalmers opted to go for the ice-cream in the hope that Mr. Purdie would want to accompany her? The thought sickened her for she did not feel that her idol would be capable of such cunning. In that case, it was her father who needed protection.

Miss Chalmers a schemer? It was unthinkable. She dismissed the thought as unworthy and felt ashamed for having allowed it into her mind. Even as it went, however, it was replaced by another. Was it just coincidence that they had all arrived at Loch Darroch today? Miss Chalmers had been before and she had spoken with her father last night. Had they arranged it?

But if that were so, why had her father not told her?

Jane knew a sickening sense of exclusion which soured her re-discovered happiness. She had a sinking feeling in the pit of her stomach, and the inner disquiet intensified as she asked herself why her father and Miss Chalmers were taking so long with the ice-cream, if they had only to go to the top of the lane and over to the car park. Surely, they could not have walked to the adjoining village.

She did not have her watch with her but it seemed like an eternity since they had gone.

Miss McTurk, on the garden lounger, seemed intent on frying herself. Quietly, Jane rose to her feet, slipped on her flip-flops and, still in her bathing costume, made her way up the lane. She expected at each bend to encounter them and she was ready with her little excuse—that she wondered if they needed help. But she reached the road without seeing them. There, in the car park stood a mobile ice-cream van, a little queue of people beside it, but no Mr. Purdie, no Miss Chalmers.

A little further along the road a signboard indicated a tea-garden, and some sixth sense told Jane that her quest would end there. The inhibition which had immobilised her in the caravan the previous evening had lowered its threshold. She knew that she had a choice of returning to the shore or of giving rein to the hot desire which sought to penetrate the web which was weaving itself slowly but surely round her father and Miss Chalmers. Instinctively, she knew that the satisfaction of her curiosity would entail pain, self-inflicted, but the need to explore the mystery clamoured with an insistence that was not to be denied. She did not know what she expected to find but find it she must. The road she trod was forbidden ground but tread it she must, though at its end she should be scorched by a burning fiery furnace. Passers-by saw a youthful teenager in a bathing suit, flip-flopping at a trot along the road. Not even Jane herself recognised the dynamo of long-inhibited emotion which propelled her.

The tea-garden was surrounded by a fence, inside which was a border of evergreens spaced at fairly close intervals. Further in again, some rambling rose-trees twined their arms in a series of floral arches all round the garden. In the middle, a small fountain sent a shimmering cascade of water on to the water-lilies floating on the surface of the pond. There were tables and chairs, some with gaily coloured sunshades.

Jane peered through the fence from first one viewpoint and then another, but there was either a bush or a table in the way. She moved to the opposite side of the garden. She was determined to see.

And there they were, only yards from the fence, seated at one of the little tables, in light-hearted conversation with each other. Miss Chalmers was smiling. So was her father. They seemed absorbed in each other and were oblivious of the observer's presence.

Like an expelled cherub, Jane looked hungrily over the fence, between the bushes and through the archway of roses at the couple, who for the moment had taken the stage in yet another scene of the divine drama. She could not hear what they were saying, but the murmur of first one voice, then the other, reached her. The casually lowered tone suggested an intimacy which stabbed her to the heart, and she surrendered to the knowledge, with a bitterness hitherto unknown in her short life, that her father loved Miss Chalmers. She shared his feeling and had accepted it only so long as she had felt herself to be the pioneer in their joint venture. It was she, not Madge nor Fiona, who had uncovered the treasure. It was she who had held the pearl aloft for their disinterested inspection. It was she who had led her father to the shrine, she who had been the high priestess of the new cult in which she had seen him as a mere acolyte. But he had thrust her on one side, defied her mediation, ignored the taboos and entered the sanctuary.

And the skies had not fallen. The goddess who Jane had felt must be worshipped at a respectful distance had opened the door to the intruder, and had smiled upon him with a welcome which had not been vouchsafed to Jane.

Did the goddess love the acolyte who had stepped beyond his appointed station to claim equality with herself? Jane searched the serene, untroubled face, the warm expression in the eyes, the smiling lips, and in them read her own doom.

She who had been first in her father's life and sole votaress in the new religion had been supplanted. Her new and degraded status was unacceptable but she must accept it. Her demotion to second best was intolerable but she must tolerate it.

She did not move. She could not. Once more, inhibition took over and prevented the rush of tears which would have brought relief.

Only when Miss Chalmers and her father rose to their feet did she alter her position, but then it was to change her vantage point. Hand in hand, they took a stroll round the garden between the rose arches and the bushes, still speaking in low-toned voices, occasionally halting as though to clarify a point; sometimes, it seemed, simply to look and look and look with endless pleasure, each on the other.

Jane fled.

***

"Sorry we've taken so long," said Mr. Purdie, as he emerged with Miss Chalmers from the lane on to the beach. "There was such a queue for ice-cream that we took a turn along the road and came back when it was quieter."

Miss McTurk took off her sunglasses and looked up lazily.

"Patience is a virtue," she said sententiously, "and virtue brings its own reward. Everything comes to those who wait, eh, Jane?"

Jane smiled a watery smile. She had hastened back to take up her position on the beach and found Miss McTurk as she had left her, on the sun-lounger, a willing sacrifice to Apollo. It seemed as though her absence had not been noticed.

From the far side of a yawning gulf, she viewed the pair who had just returned. Their utterances, as they chatted to Miss McTurk, could hardly have been described as ecstatic. Nor did they look any different, she decided, but that was surely their duplicity. Jane's own experience of love had led her to anticipate that a response from the loved one would surely infuse a degree of spring into the step, such as a kangaroo might envy; and that the resultant speech, if not in tongues, would at least be couched in poetic diction. But they seemed quite normal. Miss McTurk did not appear to notice anything. She alone had plumbed the mystery of the developing relationship.

But behind the tension which her discovery had engendered, she knew that the mystery remained—the mystery of the bastard child, of the adulterous relationship, of Joseph who refused to *lie* with Potiphar's wife, of David who *lay* with Bathsheba the wife of Uriah the Hittite, the mystery in which her father's relationship with Miss Chalmers held pride of place, the mystery which she knew instinctively was no mystery to them.

***

That evening after Jane had gone to bed, Mr. Purdie sauntered off casually for a stroll.

"Won't be long," he said as he left the van. He had often slipped out thus when they went away together and Jane was usually asleep on his return. This time, however, she knew there would be no sleep for her until he came back.

She peeped out of a corner of the window and watched him as he sauntered slowly to the gateway leading out of the caravan park. There he paused. Meanwhile, a figure emerged from the caravan at Pitch No.5 and ran lightly across the moonlit sward towards him. Momentarily, the two merged into one, then hand in hand they set off up the road.

Jane trembled. Her heart was beating too fast and the turmoil within her was almost more than she could contain. Indignation as well as misery held her in its sway, and she longed to get up, dress and pursue them.

"I felt like a walk too," she would say with feigned innocence. Then she would plant herself between them and monopolise the conversation. She would resist all persuasion to go back to bed. She needed the cool of the evening after the heat of the day, she would say.

But she knew that this was an impossible course of action. She lay down but there was no release for her. Where were they off to, she wondered. They would not walk to the village at this time of night, but would no doubt be on the lane beyond the site which led to the clachan a couple of miles further on. How long would that take? She propped herself up again on her elbow and looked out.

A depressing sense of the futility of her life swept over her though she could not have defined it as such. Though she had never consciously evaluated her affection for her father, she had functioned entirely within the framework of her relationship with him. The algebra which had taken such a compulsive hold, the declension of those fascinating Latin nouns, the French verbs which she could recite backwards, all these things which she had consciously prized had drawn their significance from the person whose significance in her life was supreme. Till now, with justification, she had unconsciously believed that the feeling was reciprocal. But now, her world had turned upside down. Because she could not be everything to him, she believed herself to be nothing.

The concept of the masculine element in relationships was a factor which had not really impinged on her consciousness. In a single-sex school, the situation did not arise. Jane had seen Miss Chalmers only with women members of staff and other pupils, and something in herself recoiled from the response which her father had apparently evoked. So there were facets in Miss Chalmers' personality which needed expression beyond the school round and her circle of women friends. Jane felt stunned.

Memories of Dorothy Reid's twitting on the day of the ink-bottle disaster returned to her. Dorothy and her cronies she had always regarded as belonging to a sinister underground movement, which sniggered at a side of life which was a closed book to herself, and for this reason she had been driven to adopt a superior attitude towards them. In some indefinable way, it now seemed that Miss Chalmers too belonged to this underground movement. She too had crossed the line and had eaten of the forbidden fruit.

If that were so, Jane could see no place for herself in Miss Chalmers' life and felt sorely betrayed.

Why didn't they come? In an agony Jane looked again towards the wood and the little ribbon of lane which almost encircled it.

No sign of them yet.

She tried to cry but could not. Life had suddenly assumed the quality of a horror film. Past and future were blotted out. Only the nightmare of the immediate present existed.

Still no sign of them.

Her back and legs burned where the sun had scorched them but a burning brand had been applied to a very tender spot in the unseen depths of her soul, and she was tormented by the flame.

Would they never come? In the stillness of the late evening hour, the caravan became a chamber of horrors for Jane and she started up from her bunk. An old dressing-gown which was several sizes too small for her hung in the little wardrobe and, donning it, she went out. There was no light in the caravan at No.5. Miss McTurk must be in bed.

She did not really want to go to the toilet block, but turned in that direction as the only option open. She shrank from the impulse which prompted her to go in search of her father, restrained by the need for self-defence. To what new revelation might she not be exposed? Despair and weariness eventually drove her out and she made her way back to the caravan. En route she saw what she would fain have avoided.

The strong square figure of her father and the slim neat figure of Miss Chalmers were at Pitch No.5. They were standing close together, very close together, outside the latter's caravan. Jane withdrew into the shadows but watched because she could not help herself. Seconds later, they stood as one.

"Goodnight, dear love," she heard her father murmur.

"Bless you," came the response.

Jane bowed her head.

***

The next day she was sick and did not rise.

"Too much sun yesterday," commented Mr. Purdie, holding her head as she vomited into a pail.

Jane lay back gasping. It was as though she had entered upon some new hell, unimagined even at the peak point of the previous night's horror. A pneumatic drill was boring its way through her head and ever so often a wave of perspiration swept over her. She was trapped in the caravan. She was a prisoner. Her father would go out with the two teachers, Miss McTurk would be given the slip and…

Had she not been overcome by this dreadful nausea, she knew, at least she hoped, that she would adopt a more aggressive policy today. No more cowering behind bushes or peeping out of windows. She would claim her place as her father's daughter and Miss Chalmers would be forced into a baffled retreat. Her father for that matter would be compelled to yield to her unspoken protestations.

From the earliest days, she had discovered her power. She dimly recalled an occasion when as a naughty child she had been dragged screaming from her grandparents' lounge by an exasperated father, intent on administering physical retribution. As he bent over her with hand upraised, she knew that she had one weapon only and she used it. She kissed the angry face and the bottom-smacking ended before it had begun. She could still remember his sudden expression of amused incredulity as he released her, and she knew that she had won. Then had followed a finger-wagging lecture as a sop to the outraged grandparents in the next room, who looked up surprised at the cessation of the yells and shook their heads at Mr. Purdie when a smiling Jane had returned to the lounge.

But deep down she knew that the paralysis which had beset her yesterday was her only possible reaction to a situation which it was beyond her capacity to cope with. Perhaps this dreadful sickness was actually a means of liberation for a mystifying complex of emotions that could find no other channel of expression.

"Have a cup of sweet tea," advised her father and she accepted it as she would have accepted anything he proposed. He stroked her hot forehead.

"I'll go down to the village and get something to settle your stomach," he said. "But meantime I think you would be better moving over to my bed—it's much shadier at that end of the caravan."

Jane rose unsteadily and he carried her sleeping-bag over. There was comfort in his suggestion, and for the moment she was prepared to renounce the lookout post at her own end of the caravan. She sank onto the pillow which he had not put away and he drew the curtains to.

"I won't be long, Jane," he said gently. "We'll just have a quiet day here."

Quiet day! But what did that mean? A supposedly quiet day, shared with Miss Chalmers, could mean all hell let loose for herself. She would not quickly forget the memory of the *quiet* walk which he had enjoyed with Miss Chalmers the previous night.

She groped for the pail and the sweet tea came up. A wave of perspiration was followed by a shiver and she felt cold and damp despite her burning skin.

"Drink this," commanded Mr. Purdie, administering his favourite remedy in an egg-cup. "Lie back and rest and I expect you'll feel much better by lunch-time."

Lunch-time! Was something planned for lunch-time?

"What's Miss Chalmers doing today?" she managed to ask.

"They're driving to the Falls of the White Crags," replied Mr. Purdie. "She thinks it will be cooler there, and they don't want to tire themselves out before their journey home tomorrow. They're both very sorry to hear how unwell you feel."

So he had already spoken to them this morning.

"Would you not have liked to go with them?" she heard herself saying. She was testing him.

There was a pause.

"It would have been very nice," he conceded, "but my place is here with you, Jane. Do you think I would leave my wee girl here alone when she's not well?"

For the moment, she was reassured. He took a folding chair from the boot of his car and placed it outside the open door of the caravan.

"I'm reading my paper, Jane," he said. "Just call me if you want anything."

And so an uneasy peace descended. For the moment, it was the old Daddy again—the Daddy who put her first in everything and for whom nothing was too much bother if it helped her. But the day would pass, Miss Chalmers would return and the evening would arrive. She could perhaps have a quiet walk herself with her father, but a reasonably early bedtime would be a must and then what would happen? Miss Chalmers' departure the following day would certainly mean a repetition of last night's moonlight meander.

This time tomorrow it would be all over. But the terrifying realisation was growing that there would only be a week's respite and that on their return home, contact between her father and Miss Chalmers would doubtless be resumed. There was no escape. She was struggling on a spit which would shortly be thrust again over the flames.

Her father, hitherto the haven to which all worries were carried, was now the very person in whom she could not confide. How tell him that she could not bear him to see Miss Chalmers, when she saw in herself such an inadequate substitute? How stand in the way of Miss Chalmers' happiness when she herself could not even begin to be a substitute? Each had something for the other which she could not supply.

The day dragged by. Jane remembered it with a shudder—the gradual return to her usual fitness and with it the necessity of playing a part, if only for a few hours; the smile of Judas from Miss Chalmers as she inquired how she was feeling; the stroll with her father which she insisted should be up by the clachan; bed, Mr. Purdie's disappearance and the previous night's agitation all over again.

***

Saturday at last. General activity at No.5. An open boot. A lowered sky-light. The withdrawal of the towel rail and the disappearance of the step. A last trip to the bins and the drain. Legs up!

Miss Chalmers was reversing the car towards the van. Miss McTurk was giving cautious hand signals. Mr. Purdie strolled over. Jane could just manage to accompany him. Ten minutes—less—and they would be away.

"That's kind of you, Mr. Purdie," said Miss Chalmers leaving her car as Miss McTurk signalled her to stop. He lifted the tow-bracket and brought the cup-shaped fitting to rest over the towball with the usual masculine scorn of the handle which made the hitching process less strenuous. Loosening the handbrake, he raised the jockey-wheel.

"Well, all good things come to an end," said Miss McTurk. "We've had a wonderful week."

"Delighted to have met you both," said Mr. Purdie, "and I'm sure Jane's grateful for her introduction to water-skiing."

Jane nodded acquiescence. Yes, she was grateful for that.

"I don't think Jane's quite herself yet," commented Miss Chalmers kindly, noting the lack of Jane's characteristic vivacity. "Keep out of the sun for a day or two."

"Until you've developed a hide like mine," added Miss McTurk, looking as though she had just returned from the tropics.

Jane smiled wanly. The ladies got into the car. It moved slowly off with the gently rolling giant following, willy-nilly, in the rear.

There was a chorus of goodbyes in which Jane joined in spite of herself. And they were gone. Mr. Purdie looked pensive.

Suddenly, Jane felt better but she still needed a booster.

"Daddy, let's go water-skiing again," she suggested.

Chapter X
The New Term

It was the morning interval. Miss Kelvin entered the staffroom with a sheaf of examination papers in her hand.

"Their heads are 'bloody but unbowed'," she greeted her colleagues cheerfully, laying the papers on the table. Miss Jackson handed her a cup of coffee.

"Another examination over, Miss Kelvin?" she inquired.

"Yes, IIA have just made their first incursion into deponent verbs," replied Miss Kelvin with a smile. "Thank you, Miss Mason, two sugars. It was quite a stiff paper but they're clamouring for the results. Milk, Miss McTurk? 'Will you be correcting them at the weekend, Miss Kelvin? asked Madge Stevenson'. Bless my soul, they don't think it's mid-term for the teacher as well as themselves."

"It's a very keen class, of course," commented Miss Mason of the French department. "What a fuss my IIIB made when I told them they were to be tested next week. Said they were exhausted after their English and Science papers. 'Exhausted!' I said. You have each only one paper to write. I have thirty to mark."

"IA have made heavy weather of their Geometry paper," sighed Miss Jackson. "I had to read them the riot act. 'If this is the best the A's can do,' I said, 'heaven help the C's'."

"They're at such a difficult age, your teenagers," commented Miss McKirdy of Primary 4 mildly. "Growing girls with so many adjustments to make."

"Every age is a difficult age," retorted Miss Craig grimly. "It's just that the difficulties vary with each stage of development."

There was a pause. Miss Craig had an embarrassing fashion of hinting from time to time that her own life had not been of the easiest, but she never allowed anyone close enough to find out what the difficulties had been.

"Oh, yes, I *am* sorry for them," replied Miss Kelvin more gently, "though I'm sure none of them would believe it. Take Jane Purdie, for example. She doesn't look very happy at the moment and her work has certainly deteriorated."

"I've noticed that too," commented Miss Mason. "She seems to be away in a dream most of the time, and if you call her by name she looks so startled."

"I found her wandering around Queen's Road alone at lunchtime the other day," said Miss Caskie. "She had no business to be out of the school grounds and I told her I would have to report her to Miss Chalmers, her Register Teacher. I had her for the last period that day and her eyes were very red. I felt like a villain because she's such a model pupil."

"Is anything wrong with Jane Purdie, Miss Chalmers?" asked Miss Kelvin, as the latter entered the room burdened with exercise books.

Miss Chalmers laid down the exercises before replying.

"I think she's going through a difficult phase at the moment," she replied noncommittally. "I had to reprimand her the other day for being out of school grounds during the lunch break and she burst into tears."

"I think a few repentant tears would help a girl like Dorothy Reid," commented Miss Jackson with unusual grimness. "She's been so spoiled at home that she will not accept discipline, and as for her work—"

Conversation drifted. Coffee cups rattled. The names of the brightest and the dullest made the headlines. Classroom anecdotes were exchanged. Finally, the bell rang signifying the resumption of classes and the staff dispersed. The interval was over.

***

Miss Chalmers returned to her classroom. She had no class for another forty minutes and had decided to spend the time on correction. IIA had had a test the previous day, and she was anxious to correct their papers before her attention was claimed by the accumulated efforts of her other classes.

She liked and knew IIA well, having already taught the girls the previous session. With certain exceptions, they were a bright class and competition maintained a high standard.

She turned her attention to the first paper. It was Angela Brown's. The questions covered scansion, figures of speech and the first two Acts of *As You Like It*. Angela was average to bright and her writing, like herself, had a gangling quality. It was a good paper.

Dorothy Reid. Mmmh... Dorothy could be average if she tried but she lacked application. Had confused Anapaest with Dactyl and couldn't spell either of them. Obviously, had given no real thought to the Shakespeare, however well she had elocuted it in class. She did not really merit her position in an A class.

Madge Stevenson, Jean Dunne, Monica Maclean, Fiona Ross, Nancy Young. The standard of performance varied but the content of most papers indicated a grasp of the work.

Jane Purdie. Miss Chalmers hesitated before reading her paper. Jane's work had not been up to her usual standard this term and she had been inattentive in class. It was not the inattention of the daydreamer, who had on occasion to be summoned back to reality and whose usual response to correction was a mischievous grin of acknowledgement. It was an unhappy withdrawal, not only from work but also, she had noticed, from social contact. She no longer integrated with the class. She tended to keep her eyes lowered when she walked along the corridor. For the most part, she avoided Miss Chalmers' eye.

Miss Chalmers had been pleasantly conscious during her years of teaching of her personal influence over her pupils. Both in the co-educational school and at Earlswood she had been aware of her popularity and she had used it constructively. Her normal reaction to the frank gaze of a teenager was a friendly smile which usually evoked a similar response. It had been thus with Jane Purdie last session.

This term, however, Jane had kept her eyes on the floor, when she should have been looking towards Miss Chalmers. The occasional question did not elicit a consistent lack of concentration and she therefore judged it best to refrain from criticism. At other times, however, when each girl's attention was focussed on her own individual textbook, she would find Jane staring at her with an expression which searched and wondered and speculated. At first she had not attached undue importance to the scrutiny, but when her own smile had evoked only the feeblest response, she found it increasingly difficult to maintain a cheerful mien. Once or twice, in fact, she had herself been unable either to smile or to retreat behind a corrective. For seconds, her eyes had met Jane's, and it was Miss Chalmers' expression which had searched and wondered and speculated.

She had become anxious and her anxiety was now heightened by Miss Kelvin's question. Had there been general discussion about Jane before she had entered the room? Until Miss Caskie had reported the lunch-time incident the other day, she had not known whether Jane's deviant behaviour had even been obvious to other members of staff.

She glanced through Jane's paper. No, this was not the Jane Purdie who had topped the English class last session. She closed her eyes and rested her head despairingly on her hands. If the rest of her work was no better, further concern would be shown. She knew only too well the reason for the change in Jane, but how could she face confrontation by her colleagues? As Jane's form teacher, the onus would be on her to look further into the matter.

That she loved George Purdie deeply, she knew beyond a shadow of doubt. That she had acted against her better judgment in allowing the relationship to develop she also knew, though the factors causing the present crisis were poles apart from those which had given rise to her original inhibition. The circumstances of her life had actuated her distrust of men. The anxiety engendered in a child whose affection she had previously commanded could not have been foreseen.

Her return home from her caravan holiday had brought her face to face with the realities of her life as she had lived it over the previous few years, and in the week which intervened before the return of the Purdies she had had time to take stock of the situation. At one level, she wished that she had never met George. At another, that the whole matter could be dismissed as a holiday romance. But at a deeper level still she needed the reassurance that she was loved and wanted as a woman, and she tremulously awaited his first phone call.

Yes, he telephoned her. Could they meet? And with the ball back in her court she temporised—perhaps to test his sincerity, perhaps as a last gesture of self-defence, as a token rejection of herself lest the greatly feared alternative should recur. The relationship could be halted at this stage, she knew, relegated like a holiday snapshot for future retrospective enjoyment. Consent to see him on home ground, and the relationship would immediately establish itself as an integral part of her life.

She hesitated for a week, during which he telephoned her four times. She hesitated for a week, though hopeful that her refusals would not be accepted. At the end of the week, he sounded so discouraged that her heart smote her. She agreed to meet him. As the new term was still a week away, she told herself, as a sop to her fear of involvement, that the outing could still be regarded as part of her holiday. They had a meal together and a stroll in one of the city parks. It was an evening out of time, when they looked with a new perspective on the streets of the city where they both worked and saw it transformed. Thus, she had dated Alastair and Hector, and she hesitated at the end of the evening to arrange a further meeting.

School re-started and again he telephoned her suggesting an outing. This time she told herself that her purpose in meeting him was to talk the matter through and to put it to him that with the resumption of school, she had no place in her life for a man.

Those words were never spoken. As he pulled squarely on the oars of the rowing-boat in a suburban park, she knew that in George Purdie she had met someone who would not have committed himself thus far, without full awareness of the possible outcome and the readiness to take responsibility for his actions. She compared him meditatively with Hector and Alastair. He lacked Hector's artistic leanings, but the temperament that went along with them was also conspicuously absent. He lacked Alastair's facile confidence, but he had an instinctive appreciation of her own insecurity. She knew from his devotion to Jane that he was a man of feeling and principle. His brief account of Elspeth's ill-health indicated his constancy as a husband. He was intelligent and well-informed and she loved him.

Then followed a month of mutual happiness for long unknown to either. Friday night was date night mainly because it was Jane's Guides night, and she had been accustomed to having tea with Madge Stevenson and returning to Madge's home afterwards.

***

For Jane, the comparative enjoyment of the second week at the Glen had been followed by a return of the former uneasiness. Daily she wondered how long it would be before she would be required to face the evidence of a continuing relationship. Her father was home each evening as usual, there were no phone calls that she knew of and the first week passed without incident with Madge for company.

Despite the friendly atmosphere in the Stevenson home, Jane felt herself to be operating within a vacuum, rendered the more distressing by the inner agitation which she felt unable to confide to anyone. She could not believe that her father would not be seeing Miss Chalmers again but the apparent inaction was disturbing, as was the accompanying silence between them on the subject.

She longed for the resumption of school not, as formerly, in order to look day by day upon the face of her idol, but with the half-formed hope that daily contact with both parties would enable her to put a finger on the pulse of the developing situation, and either to adjust to it or to make some attempt to control it. Of this she was only dimly conscious. What she did feel day by day was a growing desperation over the next move—what, where and when. To spot it, she must maintain constant vigilance, like a blockaded early settler who knows full well that lurking in the nearby foothills are hostile Indians, who will sooner or later send a volley of flaming arrows into the stockade. The move would come and she must be ready for it.

With the resumption of Guides on the second Friday after her return, some sixth sense told her that the arrow had been launched, and by the close of the evening, she knew that it had landed.

"I'll call for you at Madge's," said her father before leaving for the office. Would he be home for tea as usual, or was her absence at the Guides to be used as a screen for his first meeting with Miss Chalmers? Deliberately, she left her beret at home when she set out to spend the day with Madge after breakfast. She must have an excuse for returning home between teatime and Guides.

"I've forgotten my beret," she said, having changed into her Guide uniform in Madge's bedroom. Mr. Stevenson ran her home.

Normally, her father would have returned by this time but there was no response to the bell and she had to let herself in.

The arrow, which had been shot from its bowstring earlier in the day, soared flaming through the sky and now started on its downward swoop. With George Purdie's arrival at the Stevensons' a full half hour later than usual with apologies for the delay and a quiet radiance in his eyes, it rasped into the wall of the stockade with a sickening thud. The flames darted along the shaft and licked the walls.

There had been no further crosses on the calendar since the eve of the Purdies' holiday. As twilight crept in on the sixty-second day, Jane knew none of the delicious tremors of excitement which she had anticipated as she pencil-crossed her way through the July page of her calendar, with the hopelessness of an imprisoned Samson. The first day of term dawned instead like the Day of Judgement.

The chatter of Madge and Fiona fell on her ears meaninglessly as they made their way to school. Her heart hammered painfully, her school case which contained nothing but her pencils seemed intolerably heavy, and her feet carried her along as though she were an automaton. Mechanically, she returned the greetings of her friends. Yes, she had had a lovely holiday. In the caravan, up north, and she had learned to water-ski. Yes, it had been difficult to start with until someone—someone had shown her how to do a deep-water start.

The bell had rung summoning them to Assembly and the classes had filed into place. Chattering tongues continued to chatter, forgetful for the moment of the customary silence expected in the school chapel. Yes, there were Miss Kelvin, Miss Caskie, Miss Peters and a host of other supportive personalities, whose re-appearance after a period of holiday obscurity would normally have been a source of tremendous pleasure. With the betrayal, however, by the one who had been elevated to the corner-stone position, the structure had fallen and Jane looked out upon a sense of desolation.

Miss Chalmers entered along with Miss McTurk and took her seat in the transept. Gazing once more on the tranquil even features, Jane found herself wondering helplessly what diseased connection there could be between this quietly beautiful woman, and the tempestuous emotions in herself of which she was the apparent cause. Her mind juggled with the problem. If Miss Chalmers was kind and lovely, she could not bring unhappiness to anyone; therefore, argued Jane, everything must really be all right. She had only imagined her unhappiness. Actually, then, she was very happy. But her logic could not withstand the reality of the past few weeks, which thrust itself forcibly on her attention. She had been through the flames of hell and Miss Chalmers had caused it. So Miss Chalmers was herself evil. But...

"Let us with a gladsome mind
Praise the Lord for He is kind.
For His mercies aye endure,
Ever faithful, ever sure."

Chorused the girls but Jane did not join in the singing. She had prayed for succour on the night of her father's first moonlight walk with Miss Chalmers, and God had not paid any attention. Perhaps He had not heard. Perhaps

He did not exist. Perhaps He was on Miss Chalmers' side—Miss Chalmers who was evil. But God was good. Therefore, Miss Chalmers must be good. How then could she be the agent of the devil, as surely she must be, for who else could have injected the poison into the situation?

Later that day, she encountered Miss Chalmers on the corridor near the staff-room, and received the usual smile of greeting. Her response was mechanical.

Friday again came round and another arrow outlined an arc in Jane's sky before hitting its target late on Friday evening. And the Friday after and the next after that.

"Is anything worrying you, Jane?" asked George about three weeks after their return. He had noticed that Jane had been unusually quiet since their holiday.

Jane shook her head. Not for worlds would she have acknowledged her anguish or the source of it.

"I've got a lot of new lessons to learn," she said importantly. "I've got to work very hard."

George paused before putting his next question.

"How's Miss Chalmers?" he asked.

The inquiry cut her to the quick. Why had he not told her that he was seeing Miss Chalmers? Did he not know that she had eyes in her head, and could read the progress of his romance as clearly as though he had emblazoned it on the wall in letters of fire! Surely, he must sense her acute embarrassment when he apologised each week to the Stevensons for his lateness in calling for her with the excuse that he had been 'seeing a friend'.

There was the sudden appearance of After-Shave lotion in the bathroom and the unaccustomed bath on Thursday evening. There was the disappearance of his toothbrush and the toothpaste on Friday morning, and their re-appearance the same night, and there was Mrs. McSporran's querulous comment that her da was gettin' through an awfy lot of shirts these days. At every turn, it seemed, she was being confronted with the existence of an element in her father's relationship with Miss Chalmers that she could not accept. She recalled how closely they had stood outside Miss Chalmers' caravan. He must have kissed her then and perhaps at other times. He must still be kissing her. That was why he took the toothpaste with him.

She had seen this often enough on the TV screen and loftily considered it rather silly. There had in any case been an abstract quality about the celluloid love-making which had failed to convey its actuality. From time to time, there had been certain films which she had not been allowed to watch and she had accepted the prohibition without question, mentally pigeon-holing them with the stank and sewer mysteries that Dorothy Reid & Co. liked to snigger at. The thought that her father of all men should want to indulge in this silly activity and that Miss Chalmers should like it filled her with revulsion.

Her thoughts turned unaccountably to her mother, who had left them such a long time ago now and whom in a sense she had forgotten. Soft and sweet and loving. This was how Jane remembered her. Mum who had loved her so much and had wanted her to have brothers and sisters. Mum who had always been warm and plump and cosy and then was suddenly ill and was whisked away to hospital with a terrifying clanging of ambulance bells, and she had been left with Mrs. Gray next door because Daddy had gone with her. There had been whisperings in her presence between husband and wife and voices hastily lowered when she came into the room, and Daddy had looked sad and had told her that after all she would not be having a little brother or sister. It had happened many times. Then, Mum would come home and she was even sadder than Daddy and would cry and cry. That had made Jane cry too and Daddy had been so busy comforting Mum that he had not always been able to take Jane on his knee. Mrs. Gray had taken her instead and she had been frightened because she thought Mum was going to die, but when Mrs. Gray took her home again, she was even more frightened, because Mum was so white and quiet and sad that she hardly recognised her and wondered if it was someone else.

Daddy had told her that she must be a good girl and help him to look after Mum, but it wasn't easy to do this because Mum didn't want to lick the lollipop that she bought for her, or to see the worm that she had found in the garden, or to listen to the verses that she recited for her benefit.

Sometimes, Mum had talked about the babies she might have had or the babies she might still have. Jane found this intensely interesting. Mum had told her that the babies lived in her tummy until it was time for them to be born. She had even let her touch the big fat tummy when the baby was kicking so Jane knew that it was alive.

"Mum… Mum…" she said aloud one Friday night after the Guides when she had gone to bed. It was the first time she had uttered her name thus since her death.

She was confident that her mother had not been silly or nasty or evil like Miss Chalmers. She was either busy having a baby and needing careful medical attention or she was sad because she had lost her baby and needed careful medical attention.

No, Mum would do nothing silly. God sent her babies because she was so nice and because there was such a nice Daddy to help her bring them up. Thus Jane had reasoned it out and when she asked, puzzled, why God had not allowed them to be born, Mum would look sad for a moment, then give Jane a cuddle, saying, "I don't know, dear, but see what a good job He made of *you*." And that made Jane feel very important indeed.

In recent months, she had pondered a great deal on the mystery of pregnancy and birth. Despite some basic instruction at school on the facts of plant and animal life, it had not occurred to her to apply this knowledge to the human field. She had learned of the biological role of the male as outlined in the botany and zoology lessons without a great deal of interest—the exploits of Wallace and Bruce had claimed her attention at that point—and when Miss McTurk drew comparison with the human animal, she had decided that this referred to the institution of marriage and the function of the male as breadwinner. The birth of the baby was by decree of the Almighty through His knowledge of the marriage in His church.

But… there were a number of buts, which for a time she had relegated to the back of her mind for resolving at a later date. As time passed, however, she came to realise that knowledge was not the prerogative of maturity but was held in varying degrees by certain of her classmates.

There was the fact of childlessness. Mrs. Gray, with whom she had spent many happy hours of her holidays, had confided to her with a sigh on one occasion that she would have liked a little girl just like herself. She had decided at one point that Registry Office weddings were for those who did not want babies, or had been chosen by those who were not aware that marriages thus solemnised would be unfruitful. Yet Mrs. Gray, in response to Jane's question, had said she had been married in the Parish Church.

Then there was the varying size of families and her own mother's failure to have more than one live baby.

"You've got a lot of children, haven't you?" she said tentatively to Mrs. McSporran who was cleaning the cooker.

Mrs. McSporran had sighed reflectively.

"I had as many as the Lord meant me to have," she had answered piously and had gone on to polish with redoubled vigour, or so it had seemed to Jane.

Mrs. McSporran's granddaughter, who was not married, had now given birth to her child and this had also given rise to a grand-motherly sigh.

"She's been very foolish," had been her comment, "but she's learned her lesson."

Jane noticed that people tended to sigh when they spoke of the babies they had had or the babies they had not had. But why had God given Selina McSporran a baby in her unwedded state and where had the foolishness come in on Selina's part?

The bodies of some women, Jane decided, like Mrs. McSporran, having seen action once, seemed to continue automatically until... Well, had *she* stopped having her own babies because she had taken someone else's? These foster-children, for example. Perhaps Mrs. Gray had given too much of her time to Jane. That was sad for Mrs. Gray though good for Jane.

Then there were the single sex families like the Kerrs with their three boys and the Bells with their four girls. Did the body tend to go on producing what it found it was good at producing, and did it take a specially versatile mother to adjust to the production of both sexes? Madge had a sister but Fiona had two brothers, yet Mrs. Stevenson, as the kindlier mother, must surely have found more favour than Mrs. Ross in the eyes of the Lord. Mrs. McSporran, as the classic example of motherhood, had had four of each, and her sons and daughters had been born alternately, so the machinery must have needed regular readjustment.

She recalled how their minister from the elevation of his pulpit had challenged his congregation.

"What would you say to your children," he demanded, "if they asked you about their origins?"

Arm upraised he delivered his response, with all the authority of an Old Testament Prophet.

"Tell them they came from God!" he cried. "It is the best answer you can give them."

Clearly, Jane decided, the minister's views coincided with her own, but...

She thought wistfully of the woman who had only managed to produce one live baby. Mrs. McSporran may have been more successful than her mother in the art of making babies, but the memory which she retained of her mother was of a woman possessed of infinite gentleness, of refined tastes and a spiritual awareness wholly lacking in the worthy domestic, so perhaps the reproductive faculty was not the only thing that mattered.

Her thoughts returned to Miss Chalmers, whom she had loved so dearly and whom she knew she still loved. The parent-teacher relationship, with herself as the focus, had been the source of enormous pleasure, but she had been cut to the quick by the exclusive element which dominated the new relationship and by the instinctive awareness that her own unsolved mystery was at the heart of it.

***

"Does Jane know we've been out together?" asked Alison at the end of their first month of meetings.

"No, Alison, I haven't mentioned it," replied George. They were circling round together at the Thomson Dinner-Dance Centre. For George, it was the reliving of his youth. "She hasn't the least idea. I thought I would wait for a bit."

He hesitated to say why he was delaying the introduction of the subject. He wanted to ask Jane how she would feel about having another mother but could not until he was sure that Alison was prepared to marry him. Instinctively, he knew that she was a woman who could not be hurried and for the moment he was content to savour his new found happiness. Anyway, this was only their fourth outing together. He was not deceiving Jane.

Alison hesitated before speaking again. Jane was very quiet these days and avoided her gaze. Alison was sure that she knew more than her father guessed, but was reluctant to advise how the matter should be handled. How suggest that Jane should be fully apprised of the developing situation when George had not even spoken of marriage, though she felt sure it was in his mind?

And so they drifted into the second month of their courtship, unaware that the lid was about to blow off the kettle because the pressure inside had become too great to be contained.

Chapter XI
The Long, Long Trek

It was early November. Saturday evening saw George Purdie as usual at his fireside. Jane was in bed. The fire was dying but the night was not cold and there seemed no need to replenish it. Normally he would have been dozing but tonight he had been more than usually wide awake.

Only twenty-four hours previously, he had confessed his love to Alison, had told her that he wanted her as his wife and wished to court her on that basis. It was the only honourable approach, but he gave her to understand that he did not expect her to commit herself at this stage. From her response, he knew that he had sounded the right note. She needed time.

At the same time, he was worried about Jane, whose silences he had begun to feel could no longer be accounted for by her schoolwork.

He must speak to her about his meetings with Miss Chalmers. Perhaps, indeed, although he could not hope for an immediate answer from Alison, she had come into his life at the right moment for Jane's sake. He had done all he could, as a father, for her, but he was aware of his limitations and Jane needed a mother. He was glad that there was a possibility of Alison's filling that role since Jane was so fond of her. She had certainly mentioned her name very little since the holiday, but perhaps that was because she was growing up. Perhaps the holiday had given her the realisation that Miss Chalmers ate, slept, drove and holidayed just like other people. He could not help smiling at his reasoning. The holiday had certainly not brought that realisation to himself.

Saturday morning had seen the usual round of weekend shopping and in the afternoon Jane had retired to bed with a headache. No need to discuss the matter tonight. Tomorrow, after church, he would mention it.

But the next morning Jane had declined to get up. She did not look unwell but said she would like to stay in bed until lunch-time. It was Communion Sunday. George Purdie was an elder and, having satisfied himself that Jane was not ill, he set off for church.

It was his custom to be in church well before the commencement of the service. He liked the stillness that reigned before the arrival of the congregation when he could review the content of the week that had passed, anticipate in thought the week that was to come and place both against the backcloth of eternity. Only in this way could he see in true perspective the sunny uplands of life and its morasses. Only in this way could he maintain a balance when the ground seemed to be shifting under his feet. He liked especially the entry of the organist who, through the medium of music, assisted the emergent spiritual world to become a reality. There was therapy in those moments, short-lived as they were, for close on the organist's arrival came the bulk of the congregation. The other world receded before the cheerful platitudes of their greetings and subsequent chatter. The organ swell sounded in vain. No one was listening.

It was the same during the offertory. Tongues burst loose from the unnatural restraint imposed by the first half of the service. News which could not wait was exchanged.

Mr. Purdie sighed. As he served the bread and wine with his brother elders to the presently silent congregation, he decided, not for the first time, that it was difficult to see the Holy Catholic Church in the exclusive social club which passed for its current representative.

He hurried home to Jane after the service, glad of an excuse to escape from the knots of people who had gathered on the pavement outside the church.

Having quietly let himself in, he tiptoed to her room. To his surprise, the bed was empty and the covers had been thrown back. He called to her but there was no reply. A few seconds' search of the four-apartment bungalow was sufficient to reveal that she was not in the house.

Perhaps she had felt ill and had called on Mrs. Gray, but a quick telephone call ruled out this possibility.

Mr. Purdie put a match to the gas below the potatoes which he had peeled before going to church, and telephoned first Madge's mother, then Fiona's, but without the desired result. Anxiety seized him, accompanied by the presentiment that a crisis situation was in process of developing. Suddenly, he knew that it was linked with the changes which he had noticed in his daughter over the last two or three months, and his heart smote him that he had not probed into the reasons.

Her school hat and gabardine were missing from the hallstand, but more worryingly still was the bicycle which no longer stood in the usual place beside his car in the garage.

Overcoming an initial reluctance, he telephoned Miss Chalmers and within minutes he realised that she had made his anxiety her own.

An hour later, his dinner still uneaten, he telephoned the police but the Duty Officer, though not unsympathetic, tended to make light of the incident and would not accept at such an early hour in the afternoon that Jane was a missing person.

The drizzle which had been falling since his return from the Church now became a regular downpour and his alarm increased. Leaving a note addressed to Jane on the table and having alerted Mrs. Gray, he set off in his car, though without any very clear idea of where he was going.

***

Jane's feet made an endless series of circles as they pedalled automatically along, and her ears became attuned to the continual rasping contact of her tyres with the wet surface of the roads. She was cold and she was wet, through and through. The rain had been heavy for the last hour or so and had gradually penetrated the gabardine which was not intended to withstand prolonged exposure to the elements. Her socks were wet, her shoes were filled, the hair below her hat was damp and straggled in rats' tails at the side of her face and over her forehead. Her hands, which had been warm at the outset of the journey, had quickly become cold as she sped through the keen November air. Exercise had eventually restored circulation to the numb fingers gripping the handlebars, but heavy rain had seeped through the woollen gloves which now clung, sodden, to hands which had long since surrendered their hard-gained warmth.

Over the previous week or two, Jane's withdrawal from life had become almost complete. She had suffered an inner collapse from the strain of what amounted to mental supervision of her father's movements, and of daily contact with a woman whom she no longer knew whether she loved or hated. Silent speculation over the future and her inability to communicate her anxieties had taken their toll. Circumstances had not changed. The triangular relationship continued. Two days previously, on her return from school, something within her told her that she had come to the end of her tether. Subconsciously, she was groping towards the realisation that a fourth element must be introduced into the situation. She could no longer continue to take the strain alone.

The memory of her mother which of recent weeks had so vividly thrust itself up into her consciousness had been latterly accompanied by vague recollections of Aunts Grace and Isabel, her two maternal aunts. Prior to her mother's death, there had been sporadic contact, and following the funeral they had called on their brother-in-law. Jane remembered her aunts only in outline, like the ghosting figures in a television screen emerging from behind the central character which was her mother. But, sadly, it was her mother who now played no more than a ghostly part in her life. Aunts Grace and Isabel, though living in the shadows so far as Jane was concerned, must be sought out and summoned from obscurity into the foreground, where Jane was now fighting a losing battle. Surely, the partnership between her father and Miss Chalmers would no longer be able to withstand her when she confronted them flanked with reinforcements, a maternal aunt standing behind her on either side.

Aunt Isabel, she knew, lived in Helensburgh, and Aunt Grace in Clydebank. Christmas cards were exchanged every year. Occasionally, she and her father had driven through Helensburgh but George had never shown any inclination to call on Aunt Isabel. For a cyclist, however intrepid, Helensburgh seemed as remote as the imagined personality of the lady who lived there. Clydebank sounded more accessible—did not Glasgow stand on the Clyde?—and so, although she had not the slightest idea how to get there, Jane resolved to make for Aunt Grace's home.

She jotted down the address from her father's address book and took a quick look at one of his road maps. No, that was not much help with its network of red, blue and yellow lines. What she needed were precise directions. The street map! Yes, that was it, and High Elm Drive actually appeared in the index. She studied it carefully. All you had to do was to get into Glasgow and then follow one of these main roads going west. She slipped the street map into her cycle bag and closed the garage door quietly. No, not even Mrs. Gray had seen her.

There was no pleasurable anticipation in her heart as she free-wheeled down the road. She had forgotten what it was like to be light-hearted. Anxiety had brought about the disintegration of her personality. The ego had lost command and in the resultant anarchy, fear and despair ruled triumphant. An earthquake had caused the ground below her feet to open up and the familiar props had crumbled. She was beyond reason and could only grope instinctively and blindly towards a new security.

Tomorrow had no meaning for her, because she could not assess in practical terms the effect of an unknown aunt's intervention. Nor was she capable of considering her father's reaction to her desertion of him. If she were touched by any factor other than her own overwhelming need of support, it was by the negative consideration that her flight might in the first instance precipitate a closer rapport between her father and Miss Chalmers. Only this gave her momentary pause as she closed the gate behind her. But the anguish of her lonely struggle re-asserted itself, and she knew that she must retreat from a front-line position which was no longer tenable. The wounded self screamed for the application of a remedial balm. In her desperation, Jane saw Aunt Grace as a healing angel.

As she cycled through suburbia into the centre of Glasgow, she was aware of a whole series of agonised sobs which sought convulsively to rise from the very pit of her stomach. She held them in check and the effort caused her to breathe more quickly. Only when the rain started did she allow her tears expression, and along with the raindrops, they coursed down her cheeks. For the most part she wept silently for she had a horror of attracting attention, but occasionally, when the road seemed deserted, she allowed a sob to escape her. It was small relief, like the trickle of water which prevents the dam from overflowing but makes no appreciable difference to the water level. For the first time since that fateful week at the Glen, the tension from which she was suffering could have been channelled into tears but she was unable to yield to this luxury in public.

She cycled past the school, deliberately averting her eyes from the handsome ivy-covered building which had seen the awakening of both her intellectual and emotional life, and which now housed a Medusa whose countenance had spelt spiritual doom. She cycled past the blackened tenements of the city's Victorian past, oblivious of their decaying stonework and of the knots of people who huddled together out of the rain at the entrances. She barely felt the wash on her legs as an overtaking car or bus splashed through a puddle on the uneven road surface with the mindless blundering of a jungle denizen.

From time to time, she was obliged to stop in order to consult the pages of her street map which quickly grew sodden in the downpour. It would have been simpler if her starting point and destination had both appeared on one large page, but the route she must travel ran through several pages and these were not always consecutive. As Clydeside Road shot off the top left-hand corner of a left page and failed to reappear anywhere along the right edge of the preceding page, an appalling sense of frustration overwhelmed her so that she wanted to hurl the map in the gutter and scream for assistance. She peered through the ceaselessly falling rain at the network of unknown streets, on paper which was quickly losing its smooth freshness. Each time she did this, the saddle of her bicycle became soaked afresh, as had already happened each time she had stopped at traffic lights. She knew that she must travel west from the city centre, but the streets along which she cycled did not always correspond with their counterparts on the map. Was the map out of date? And she had to turn into side streets which did not always emerge where anticipated. At one terrifying point, she entered a one-way street at the wrong end and found no fewer than four vehicles bearing down on her. She dismounted, frightened by the blast of horns as they sped past, the drivers irritated but unconcerned at the cyclist who tripped as she stepped off the road and fell on the wet pavement, her bicycle on top of her. She was only slightly hurt but the indignity of the fall, more than the grazed knee and the now muddy coat, prevented her for a moment or two, from doing other than lie where she had fallen and sob aloud. Unconsciously, she equated the encounter with the strong downstream currents in the river of her own life. The rain continued to fall, seeping in between her hat and the collar of her coat. A shiver caused her to turn her attention from her emotional anguish to the wretchedness of her physical state, and she stumbled to her feet, pushing her bicycle to an upright position. No further traffic had entered the street, which Sunday and the rain had cleared of its week-day stir. No one had seen Jane in her extremity. No one

170

saw her now as she looked unhappily around her, uncertain which direction to take. She withdrew to the shelter of a close to study the street map but the sudden emergence round the bend of the stair of a shaggy-bearded, long-coated tramp with a stick in one hand and a bottle in the other caused her to flee in panic, pedalling down the street again as fast as she could.

She would fain have turned back, but she had gone so far and was so wet and lost that the effort would have been as great as that required to set her again on her westward route. It had been so easy to choose her route west out of the city, when she had been cycling west into the city and was still on familiar ground. But where was west now in this maze of dirty streets with shops that were closed and few pedestrians to approach, save those whose appearance was bedraggled and off-putting?

Then followed a dismal trek as she sought, at first vainly, to find her way back to the Clydeside Road. Lacking her usual faculty of coordination, she was slow to use the map correctly, and so urgent was her need to reach her destination that, with the inconsistency of despair, her impulse was to plunge blindly on no matter where in the mistaken belief that effort, even without direction, would eventually bring her to the desired goal.

A sudden realisation of the need for self-possession plus the seclusion of a shop doorway, at last enabled Jane to find her way back to the main road, and with a measure of relief, she pursued her way passing eventually through a whole brave new world of concrete switchbacks and archways, lined here and there with high-rise flats and flat-roofed blocks, so depersonalised a zone that it occurred to Jane in her confusion that she had perhaps arrived on another planet.

Was it possible that she at length arrived in Clydebank, numb and scarcely caring, assured of her arrival only by a dazed assimilation of the words on a church notice board?

Another consultation with the map to find her route to High Elm Drive... Suddenly, she was there and, with No.9 confronting her almost immediately, she found herself quailing at the prospect of meeting this unknown aunt who sent them a Christmas card every year, but never an invitation to tea, and who never remembered her birthday.

It was a quiet avenue consisting of sandstone terrace houses whose frontages were in various stages of cleanliness. Decisions regarding the sandblasting process had obviously been made piecemeal and over a period by the respective house-owners, so that the frontages themselves alternated from the smoke-encrusted sandstone of past years, through the returning grey of those who had pioneered the cleansing process, to the dazzling white of the recently converted.

The now dingy surface of Mrs. Oliphant's house indicated that she had been a pioneer of pioneers. Oblivious of this, Jane propped her bicycle against the wall and pushed open the gate. Awareness of journey's end brought awareness of the weariness induced by the exertion of her long ride and by spent emotion. She walked up the row of slabs at the side of the trim lawn. The lower half of the front door was of panelled wood, the upper half of opaque glass on which was traced a sinuous pattern in a variety of colours. Suddenly, excitement possessed Jane. On the other side of this door lived the sister of a dearly loved mother, but for whose death the present crisis would never have arisen. Jane had no up-to-date photographs of her aunt, and those taken in her girlhood had not been looked at for several years. At one level, she wondered apprehensively what aunt Grace would look like. At a deeper level, she wanted to see the door opened by none other than her own beloved mother.

She rang the bell. No answer.

She rang again.

There was a faint sound from within, which gradually became definable as the sound of slow shuffling footsteps. Jane's apprehension returned. Surely, Aunt Grace was not as old as that.

The rattling of a chain followed and the door opened slowly to the extent allowed by the few inches of chain, which the occupier had only just slid into position.

What Jane saw was the ghostly figure of an old, old lady who, despite the protection afforded by the chain, cowered behind the door and peered suspiciously round it. The hair was white, the face lined and wizened, and the expression indicated that the caller was not welcome.

Jane's heart sank. It was as though her whole inside dropped out. This was not Aunt Grace. This *could* not be Aunt Grace... For a moment, each stared bewildered at the other.

"I—I thought Mrs. Oliphant lived here," Jane faltered at last.

The face continued to survey her with distaste. To a tired old woman who had lost interest in life there was nothing in Jane's appearance to inspire confidence. Her face, coat and stockings were mud-spattered from her fall. Her hair hung about her face in streaky disorder. She was as uncertain of life as the old woman and her manner betrayed this. She did not look like a girl from a good school or from a home where she received care.

"Mrs. Oliphant doesn't live here any longer," muttered the old woman.

It was the last blow.

"Doesn't live here!" echoed Jane stupidly.

The door started to close.

"Oh, please!" cried Jane, darting forward. She must learn more of her aunt's present whereabouts. She reached the door just in time to prevent its closure and threw her weight against it. The old woman uttered a thin scream.

"Go away or I'll send for the police," she cried, terrified.

The police! Jane was a good girl. Dimly, she was aware that her conduct that whole afternoon had exceeded normal standards. Dimly, she was aware that brakes had to be applied by someone somewhere if she were unable to apply them herself. But the police! She saw her name in the headlines, saw an institution with locked doors, and saw herself outlawed from society. Then, for a single fleeting moment, the memory of life at home flashed into her mind and once more desperation grew strong within her.

"Yes, I'll go," she whispered to the old woman. "But please tell me where Mrs. Oliphant has gone to. I must know. She's my aunt."

There was a moment's hesitation before the old woman spoke again.

"She's gone to Paisley. Now, go away!"

Jane yielded and the door banged shut.

Paisley! Paisley!

She sank on to the doormat and tears flowed, not the anguished sobs to which she would fain have given expression earlier in the afternoon. They were the tears that followed anti-climax, tears that had to be shed before the overtaxed brain could begin to think again.

Paisley! How could she get to Paisley from here? And whereabouts in Paisley did Aunt Grace live?

With the threat of the police uppermost in her mind, she tapped politely on the door. Surely, the old woman would not deny her this information. But there was no reply. There was not even a letterbox to scream through. What did the postman do?

Next door! Surely, the neighbours would help.

But next door there was no one but a lanky youth with long hair and a prominent Adam's apple which a reluctant beard strove vainly to conceal. He tried to be helpful.

"You can take the ferry over to Renfrew and after that it's only a few miles to Paisley," he said.

He gave her directions to the ferry over the Clyde but could not supply the address. His straightforward, down-to-earth manner restored Jane's faith in herself. Now that she knew there was no need to return to Glasgow before making for Paisley, her determination to find Aunt Grace returned and she mounted her bicycle.

On the other hand, the thought of a journey by water caused her certain misgivings. It was with some hesitation that she considered the surrender of herself to another element, which not only suggested a degree of risk but also a final severance of ties with home. She had never been on a ferry and in imagination associated it with the one-man-operated rowing boat of an age that was gone. She recalled the flight by ferry from a wrathful sire of Lord Ullin's daughter and the watery grave that awaited her. She too had preferred 'the raging of the skies' to domestic difficulties. But the circumstances of the unfortunate bride of Ulva's chief were quite the reverse of Jane's. This time the flight was not *by* a courting couple but *from* a courting couple. Jane suddenly wondered if her former sympathy with the young lovers had been misplaced. Perhaps Lord Ullin had suffered as she had suffered. Perhaps he had been well rid of them both.

She knew that her attitude was warped, and tears sprang again to her eyes when she thought of her own particular Lord Ullin, who would certainly be inconsolable in his grief were his daughter to meet her end on the Yoker/Renfrew ferry.

Rain, rain, rain! It poured down relentlessly and by the time Jane had reached Ferry Road, the young man's friendly manner had receded from her mind and once more she had plunged into an unfriendly unknown limbo-land.

She free-wheeled down the short bend of Ferry Road to the river. There was certainly nothing romantic about the approaches—a tarmac road with a brick wall on one side and a respectable villa on the other, some grey huts, a turnstile, and on the other side a skip, a barrow, a brick shed and a heap of gravel. Beyond the ferry area were huge ladder-like structures of steel, looking like the equipment in a giant's adventure playground, an ugly but perhaps reassuring reminder to Jane that she was still in industrial Glasgow, ferry or no ferry.

But the biggest jolt to her romantic conception of a ferry was the ferry itself which had just left the Yoker side. Jane blinked. It was like a house. There was a broad platform for vehicles and on either side stood a one-storey structure, on the top of which were long wooden seats where passengers could take the air on a clear day. It did not remotely resemble a boat as it chugged squarely from one side of the river to the other, drawn by chains on an underground pulley system.

Jane looked over at Renfrew as at the Promised Land. She saw trees, a church spire, the white gable of a hotel, and a solid-looking house near the water's edge which might have been a fisherman's hostelry in the old days. It looked nice even in the rain. She closed her eyes to the nearby factory buildings, the discoloured boats only a few yards upstream, and the high wooden piers and platforms projecting into the water. The other side *must* be nicer than this.

Now the house was chugging across the river with its quota of cars and foot passengers, the latter sheltering in the lower part of the side structures. It reached the slipway, and there was a sudden writhing in the water as the chain surfaced. The ramp was lowered and cars and passengers disembarked.

Painfully aware that she had no money, Jane slipped aboard with the other passengers—two cyclists in oilskins, a fat woman with a see-through umbrella and a young couple with a push-chair bearing a smug-looking toddler, whose face alone emerged from the tent-like covering which swathed child and push-chair alike.

The iron gates clanged behind her but Jane was scarcely aware that the ferry was now in motion.

'The boat had left a stormy land,
    A stormy sea before her,'

murmured Jane to herself with only partial appropriateness. The river was like glass. Even the rain had slackened. With the chugging of the engine in her ears, she might have been on the lower deck of a pleasure steamer bound for Rothesay or Dunoon. She looked longingly downstream and wished that she might indeed sail away into the mist, never to return. For the brief few minutes of the crossing, she was in No-Man's-Land, a vacuum, and she wished she might stay there forever. Behind her was a father who had deceived her, a teacher who had wronged her. Ahead, hovered an unknown aunt who had never showed much interest but from whom she was now expecting a great deal.

Some flotsam floated past, perhaps, like the ferry, to ply back and forward between Renfrew and Yoker, perhaps to be washed downstream and out to sea. Flotsam, like herself.

The fat woman was looking at her curiously. She was so wan and bedraggled that she had roused the woman's compassion.

"Are you a'right, hen?" she asked.

Jane nodded. The woman reminded her of Mrs. McSporran.

"I'm going to Paisley," she replied tonelessly.

"Ah'm goin' there an'a," replied the fat woman, "but ah'm takin' the bus. It's no a day to be oot on a bike."

Jane nodded. She was wishing she could join her kindly fellow-passenger on the bus.

She looked so forlorn that the woman could not resist asking, "Are your Ma and your Da deid, like?"

The final apologetic word had a softening effect on the directness of the question, but Jane was beyond taking umbrage at its implication. She explained her problem and the woman was instantly sympathetic.

"Will your auntie have the phone, like?" she asked, again indicating with great delicacy her awareness of the personal nature of her interrogation.

Jane signified that she would have and was immediately counselled to consult a telephone directory. Not in Renfrew, added the fat woman, which was in the Scotland West Area. She must wait until she arrived in Paisley. A new directory had just been issued and it was just possible that her aunt's name would be included in its pages.

She had reached the other side and the ramp, which had been uptilted like the upper jaw of a monster, was lowered. There was a brief wash of water from beneath the ferry up the slipway and cars and foot passengers disembarked.

At the entrance to the ferry area stood the Paisley bus. The woman paused before leaving Jane.

"Have you any money, hen?" she asked. This time there was no apology for the question.

Jane shook her head and the fat woman opened her purse.

"If you want tae phone your auntie, you'll need tuppence," she said.

Jane was abashed and told the woman of the debt she had already incurred to the Clyde Port Authority, but the woman did not think it mattered and pressed the coins into Jane's hand.

"If you're in any trouble, hen," she advised, "go to the polis."

She mounted the bus.

"Ta-ta, hen," she called and the bus started off.

The rain resumed its earlier downpour. Jane, putting the coins carefully in her pocket, wearily mounted her bicycle and headed along the main road for Renfrew. By now the afternoon was well advanced and the light was showing signs of fading. She was hungry as well as weary. Emotion had evaporated. She no longer wanted to cry. She was conscious only of physical wretchedness. She was cold. She was wet. She was alone. Life was a two-wheeled pilgrimage into infinity. It seemed as though it never had been, never would be, anything else.

Road signs helped her and Renfrew, then Paisley, was reached. A telephone directory did indeed supply Mrs.

Oliphant's new address. Strange how vital information was so anonymously conveyed.

An assistant in a brightly lit cafe gave her directions. In her heart, she said thank you to the fat woman on the ferry.

Chapter XII
Jane Meets Her Aunts

Mrs. Oliphant poured herself some tea from the silver teapot which had been her mother's and took a sausage roll from the warming-stand at her feet. The tray was set for one only because Mr. Oliphant spent much of his time at weekends golfing and at the club-house, arriving home at six, seven, eight o'clock or even later.

At fifty, Mrs. Oliphant was a pale reflexion of the plump, rosy-cheeked girl of five and twenty years earlier, who had married a successful businessman. Maturity, marriage and success in her chosen career had combined to encourage the development of a character which even in girlhood had given promise of organising ability and leadership. With the fading complexion and the sharpening of contours, however, had emerged a forceful personality with a keen brain and an inexhaustible supply of energy.

Her own church background and the post-war development of the social services had not unnaturally attracted her to social work, and ambition had carried her from the original front-line fight against delinquency, up through a senior post in the probation service to the higher echelons of the generic Social Work Department, which in the late sixties replaced the individual local authority services.

Mrs. Oliphant's work played an important part in her life and, as there had been no children of the marriage, she was able to give to it her almost exclusive attention. She had long since discarded the religious beliefs of her early years and her life was now based on a practical humanitarian philosophy. Not for her the aimless domesticity of her sister Isabel with her coffee mornings, her occasional charity work and flower arrangement classes.

She was not without friends, though at one time the demarcation lines between work and social life had tended to become confused. Case Conferences at the Children's Homes had become pseudo-social gatherings, and she had become caught up in a series of evening Teach-Ins held at the homes of individual social workers, which had rapidly dropped their initial educational function.

The realisation that over-involvement with work was not the best way to keep a husband happy had led to a redirection of her thinking. A number of cheese-and-wine parties at their home had led to a considerable widening of her social circle, and she was gratified to observe that her husband also appreciated the new turn which their life had taken. She found satisfaction in displaying her talents as cook and hostess, and had the faculty of producing fairly elaborate meals at short notice.

She still had a tendency to allow her work to spill over into the evening and to regard with lofty benevolence those of her colleagues who strove, however vainly, for regular hours. As Mr. Oliphant was rarely home before seven p.m. there was no need for modification to this aspect of her work-pattern, and thus their married life found its own level of reasonable compatibility.

The sausage rolls, of her own making, were excellent, as were the jam sponge and the shortbread. Walter would enjoy them when he came home. She listened to the rain which battered the windows of the comfortably furnished lounge. There could not have been much golf today, she thought, even for an enthusiast like her husband. She suppressed the resentment which questioned his preference for the club-house to the domestic hearth.

The sound of feet on the gravel path outside attracted her attention. She was not expecting visitors and she knew it could not be Walter, who always drove his car down the side of the house and entered by the back door. She waited for the bell to ring, and when only silence followed the cessation of the footsteps at the front door, she decided to investigate.

Having switched on both the hall and vestibule lights, she opened the door. A small bedraggled figure quickly withdrew a hand from the bell, which she had hesitated in the first instance to ring.

Mrs. Oliphant stepped forward as she had always done when greeting a client. Her smile was pleasant and made her look younger.

"Yes?" she said questioningly.

Jane was well aware that this time she had arrived at the right address. She knew from the brisk efficiency of the woman's manner that this was Aunt Grace as described to her by her father, but she delayed declaring herself.

"Can I help you?" asked Mrs. Oliphant, puzzled by the child's silence.

Jane looked up into her eyes but at first did not speak. The revelation of her identity would be followed either by acceptance or rejection and she shrank from that fateful moment.

"Are you Mrs. Oliphant?" she stammered.

The smile faded and was replaced by a slight knitting of the brows which Jane interpreted as irritation. Better perhaps to announce herself and await the consequences.

"I'm Jane," she mumbled, lowering her eyes. She did not dare to view the first reaction in the woman's face. There was a pause, followed by an exclamation.

"Jane Purdie! Good heavens!"

Jane raised her eyes beseechingly.

"You'd better come in," said Mrs. Oliphant. She was discomfited by the sudden appearance of this niece whose birth she had grudged her sister, and she was struggling to regain her customary composure. She led the way back into the lounge. In its pleasant warmth, aunt and niece took stock of each other.

Elspeth over again, thought Mrs. Oliphant with some emotion. The same solemn eyes, the same lank hair, same nose, same mouth. Had she the same contrary ways, the same determination to go her own way no matter what?

"Take your wet coat off, Jane," she said, not unkindly, "and your hat. Mercy me, you're wet through."

The need to be practical held the jealous sister within her in check, but the role of aunt to which she was a stranger did not come readily. The social worker took over.

"Is something wrong, Jane?" she asked.

Jane nodded dumbly. How she was to confide in this efficient stranger she did not know. Even her nodded agreement to the question seemed like a breach of faith with her father.

"Does your father know where you are?"

A shake of the head.

"Then I think we'd better ring him," said Mrs. Oliphant decisively.

Jane nodded.

She led Jane to a bedroom and switched on the radiator.

"Take your things off, Jane," she said, "and let me see what I can find you to wear."

She rummaged in the chest of drawers and wardrobe. Jane bit her lip. Here was another difficulty. She was not accustomed to undress in front of someone else and her developing figure was causing her acute embarrassment. Momentarily, she wished she were back in the rain or out on the ferry or being washed downstream with the pieces of flotsam. It was quite as impossible to remove her clothes as it would be later to drop the veil from the intimacies of her emotional life.

"Come along, Jane," said Mrs. Oliphant, briskly approaching with an armful of dry clothes.

Jane hung her head.

Mrs. Oliphant quickly divined the situation.

"I'll run a bath for you, Jane," she said, "and I'll phone your father while you're in it."

***

Warm and dry in an ill-fitting assortment of Aunt Grace's clothing, Jane sat huddled in silent misery by the fire. Mr. Purdie had been advised of his daughter's safe arrival in Paisley, and had reluctantly agreed to allow her to stay the night.

In an incredibly short space of time, Aunt Grace had prepared a satisfying meal which had gone a long way towards restoring Jane's vitality. The recession of physical discomfort, however, had been accompanied by a return of the earlier emotional turmoil which had driven her from home. The anxiety which had been displaced by the ache of numb fingers, by wet feet and damp clothes was flooding back into consciousness. The blurred image of Aunt Grace which had sustained her throughout her wanderings had vanished before the crisp, incisive personality of the real woman. The fairy godmother who would make all well by a wave of her wand had crumpled before the efficient social worker who had fed, clothed and sheltered her, but who would at any minute now require an explanation.

Detached to some extent from the domestic situation by her new surroundings, Jane fingered her shortbread with an apparent disinterest which belied the mounting tension within her.

Mrs. Oliphant, who had hovered to and fro during the serving of the meal, had withdrawn to the spare room in order to make up Jane's bed. Now she was returning, and observing that Jane had almost finished, she sat down on the armchair opposite and opened the conversation.

How had Jane known she had moved? She should, of course, have informed Mr. Purdie of her change of address. So Jane had called first of all at Yoker! Dear me, she had cycled a long, long way.

Mrs. Oliphant knit her brows and viewed her niece with concern.

"Was there something you wanted to see me about, Jane?" she asked.

Jane did not reply. The truth in its simplicity—that her father had fallen in love with her favourite teacher—sounded too feeble an explanation to justify her flight from home, or her arrival, like a refugee, at the home of her aunt. The welter of emotion generated by her knowledge of their relationship had indeed been only too real but she had no words with which to describe it.

"Something is bothering you, Jane," said Mrs. Oliphant, reaching out for her cigarettes.

Jane nodded without raising her eyes. She knew that the moment she had unconsciously longed for since the day when her father had accompanied Miss Chalmers to the village had arrived. She had herself created it—the opportunity to express her anxiety, her indignation, her anger. The friendly ear, the ear of the aunt, of the social worker, the professional unraveller of problems, awaited the unburdening of her overtaxed emotions. But the language of everyday usage was too weak to convey the anguish of a personality divided against itself and bewildered by a situation which had become explosive through ignorance and circumstance. Impossible to pour into each word sufficient meaning to make of it a fit vehicle of expression for her torment. Between Jane and Aunt Grace, inhibition raised a wall which would have effectively silenced the oratory of a Churchill.

"Perhaps we could discuss it together," Aunt Grace was saying.

Jane raised her eyes and gazed searchingly at the face of the aunt who was a stranger to her. She did not doubt Aunt Grace's good intentions, which made her own taciturnity all the more unaccountable. But there was a professional detachment in her approach which would have compared unfavourably with the friendly helpfulness of the motor mechanic who serviced her father's car. Grace Oliphant was self-confident in her diagnostic role, and this very confidence caused Jane to cling to the misery which she had longed to unburden.

Aunt Grace, she felt instinctively, was accustomed to produce solutions out of a hat. But had she ever been asked to understand such a problem as Jane's? Perhaps it would have been easier to confide in Mrs. McSporran.

In her smart tweed skirt with matching jumper, cigarette poised between carefully manicured fingers and with one slim leg elegantly wound round the other, Grace Oliphant impressed Jane as someone who lived through her head, not her heart, who had shed her own problems, if indeed she had ever had any.

Jane longed to cry. Where had the great sobs gone which had all but choked her earlier in the day?

She wanted to say, "Help me to cry," but could not.

She had taken the initiative in seeking out Aunt Grace. Aunt Grace must make the next move. That Aunt Grace *was* making the next move, as well as she knew how, Jane did not even recognise. But how could she be expected to know, poor woman, that this was not the particular response that Jane needed.

Mrs. Oliphant arched her brows in amused incredulity. She did not quite know what to make of this niece of hers who had arrived on her doorstep like a bird with an injured wing but who was only able to hop thus far and no further. In the momentary silence, Jane felt, as though she were under the observation of an etymologist, unable to identify the strange new insect which had crawled up out of the ground.

Jane herself did not know what she wanted. The curtain of the years had descended on the events of her earlier life. Some peep-holes had allowed her to glimpse odd incidents, but she would have had difficulty in separating her own memories from the pictures created in her mind by her father's anecdotes. Of the unformed questionings and private terrors which had never reached consciousness she could have no grasp. The pattern which led from love through marriage to pregnancy, and from pregnancy to illness and death, was as firmly established in Jane's subconscious as the links of a chain forged by an infernal Vulcan. The mother from whom she had sought reassurance as a child had been enmeshed in the mystery and the secret terrors had remained unresolved. Recent events had aroused her latent fears, already responsible for the repression of sexual curiosity.

"I can't help you if you don't tell me what's wrong," said Aunt Grace with undeniable logic.

"Help me to cry, help me to cry," screamed Jane silently. The dam was full but it had turned to ice.

She hung her head. The afternoon's exploration had ended in failure. That she had hurt her father, she felt sure and she was now making a fool of herself to an aunt whose favour, under different circumstances, she would have valued. She had broken into Mrs. Oliphant's evening; she had accepted a meal, a bath and clothes, and was now about to accept a bed. The least she could do was to offer an explanation, but her lips remained silent. To her sense of guilt for having deserted her father was added the knowledge that she had made herself a nuisance to Aunt Grace. She longed to melt into nothingness.

***

She slept late the next morning. A clear, crisp day followed the rain and, emerging from sleep, Jane could feel something of a wintry chill on her face. She burrowed further into the bedclothes. Momentarily, she forgot that she was not at home till tension again gripped her, and the memory of the previous day came flooding back. She was at Aunt Grace's. She had set out from home in a desperate bid for help but had been unable to reach out for it when it had been offered. The star that had appeared in the sky had proved lustreless on closer inspection, and once more the heavens were dark. Today was mid-term. Tonight, her father would come for her. Tomorrow, she would be back at school, exactly where she had started.

Of a sudden, she heard the door of the bedroom opening quietly and the sound of soft footsteps in the room. Aunt Grace! Or perhaps Aunt Isabel. Aunt Grace had to go to work but had promised not to leave until Aunt Isabel had arrived. Jane's spirits sank even lower at the prospect of an encounter with her second aunt. In place of the succouring angels of her imagination, she now saw two birds of prey into whose nest she had somehow fallen.

She lay still, unconsciously repeating her withdrawal of the previous evening and with the bed-clothes for reinforcement. In the cocooned warmth of the bed, she was safe. Just let her remain there forever more.

The footsteps had stopped. Had her aunt withdrawn from the room or was she standing beside her bed? Jane tensed. The bedclothes no longer comforted but restricted. Because she knew she must lie still, she had an overpowering urge to move. The hip on which she was lying became unaccountably stiff and she slid round on to her back, the covers slipping from the lower part of her face.

What was that! A hand, soft and smooth, was stroking her cheek and gently pushing back the hair which straggled across her brow. She wanted to open her eyes and smile up at the owner of the hand but chose to remain detached.

"Are you sleeping, Jane?" said a voice and her eyes opened involuntarily. So this was Aunt Isabel—pink, fresh-complexioned, round and smiling. Softer, sweeter, gentler than the intellectual Aunt Grace though with a strong facial resemblance. Neither of them a bit like her mother.

Jane smiled.

"What a long sleep you've had," said Aunt Isabel, continuing to smile down at her. She had prominent white teeth, every one of which appeared to be on view. "And how are you feeling today?"

She laughed cheerfully at Jane's rejoinder.

"Come and have some breakfast," she invited, still smiling. As the morning wore on, Jane was to notice that Aunt Isabel smiled most of the time. Even when she moved about the house, her lips were parted. Perhaps, Jane decided, it was difficult for her to close her lips over these large, strong teeth.

Wearing a dressing-gown and slippers belonging to Aunt Grace, Jane followed Aunt Isabel downstairs to the living room, which was warm from the silent glow of the gas fire and as clean and tidy as a new pin. The table was set with a fresh white cloth which had a blue and yellow striped border and a place had been laid for Jane with Aunt Grace's blue-hooped breakfast set.

"You're just like your mother," smiled Aunt Isabel as she poured out the corn-flakes.

The kettle was put on and the grill lit for toast.

Her bicycle was in the garage, said Aunt Isabel. Uncle Walter had put it there last night. Her father had been on the phone this morning to inquire for her and had been told she was still asleep. Uncle Victor, her own husband, had driven her over on his way to business and she would stay till he called for her at night.

Jane was not to forget that breakfast hour quickly. It was not that her problems had disappeared. She knew only too well that they were waiting to be faced, but she had found a temporary refuge on a little rocky islet. For the moment, the tempest-tossed sea had become calm and she herself knew a degree of tranquillity.

Aunt Isabel drank some tea with her, chatting all the while. She and Uncle Victor had a roomy glass-fronted bungalow in Helensburgh on the Clyde. It had smooth white walls which they had painted together and a large garden back and front with smooth lawns and flower beds. She enumerated her flowers—rose bushes here, chrysanthemums there; borders of catmint and heather, alyssum and lobelia; daffodils, tulips, crocuses in the spring; the whole garden ablaze in mid-summer—azaleas, gladioli, poppies, sweet-peas, delphinium and marigolds, it was a riot of colour. There was overhanging pampas grass and in the background holly, cypress, even a couple of palm trees. They both spent much of their time out-of-doors, and Aunt Isabel always gave Uncle Victor his tea on the patio in summer on his return from the city, and they would sit out for the rest of the evening or take a stroll along the front as the sun went down.

Sometimes her friends would come for coffee during the day and she would throw open the French windows to let in a breath of summer. She attended classes in floral art so that she could bring her garden into the house. Victor worked so hard in town he needed beauty and quiet when he came home and she felt it was her duty to provide it.

It sounded idyllic and Jane longed to see it. In fact, she found herself wishing that she could step into Aunt Isabel's shoes, and live this life of colour and beauty, free from strain; to be, in fact—like Aunt Isabel—something of a large smiling sunflower.

During a lull, Jane felt obliged to take up the thread of the conversation and to tell Aunt Isabel something of her own life, drab though it seemed by contrast.

"We've got a caravan," she said. "We keep it in the garden and we go our holidays and sometimes for weekends in it."

It was hard to speak enthusiastically about the caravan from which, in fact, she had tended to avert her eyes since her holiday, but self-respect demanded a glowing description not only of the van itself but also of the holiday.

"Just Dad and yourself?" asked Aunt Isabel.

Jane nodded. Then, in case perhaps Aunt Isabel might think this a little dull, she added, "We met some friends there who had a caravan. Sometimes, we went out with them. It—it was lovely."

It cost Jane an effort to say this but she forced herself to smile.

"One of them taught me to water-ski," she went on. "Actually, it was one of my teachers."

"That sounds very exciting," replied Aunt Isabel. "She must be nice."

Jane voiced her agreement. After a pause she added casually, "Daddy thinks so too. He's been taking her out since then. I think they're going to get married."

Aunt Isabel could not forbear raising her eyebrows at this, but her customary smile prevented surprise from registering too markedly.

"And how will you like having a new mum?" she asked, pouring herself a cup of tea.

But Jane was unable to maintain her play-acting. Having delivered up, in a moment of composure, a confession or as near it as she could manage, her courage deserted her and the bewildered adolescent again took over.

She stared back at Aunt Isabel.

"I—I don't know," she answered, her face so full of trouble that even Aunt Isabel stopped smiling for a moment. She was out of her depth and sought refuge in her customary chatter.

"I'm sure you'll like it, Jane," she said, smiling once more. "It must have been difficult for your father over the years. I think he's made a wise decision and if it's someone you know already, that makes it easier for you."

Aunt Isabel had a comforting presence and there was a persuasive note in her voice which invited other people to share her own comfortable experience of life. Nothing had arisen to shake her out of the cosy ménage à deux which she shared with Victor. Heartbreak had not entered her experience and she found it impossible to imagine life which was lived at a different level. Anxiety need not exist so long as she could dispense coffee and little nosegays of flowers. If people's troubles were not amenable to such kindness as she could offer, there was really nothing she could do about it.

***

Mr. Purdie was a prey to conflicting emotions as he drew up outside his sister-in-law's house. Relief at Jane's safety mingled with shock that she should think of running away from home, anxiety as to the cause and irritation that she should have given his sister-in-law reason for criticising him in his single-parent role.

He was not altogether surprised in spite of the arrangements made by telephone, to find that Mrs. Oliphant had not yet returned from business. With all her efficiency, punctuality had never been one of her virtues.

Fatherly feeling was strong in Mr. Purdie, as was the governing emotion in his heart when Aunt Isabel opened the door to him, with Jane only a yard or two behind.

"My wee girl," he exclaimed with deep feeling, cuddling her close. "My own wee Jane."

The need for explanations was far from his mind at that point.

He shook hands with his sister-in-law who already had her coat on, ready for the return journey to Helensburgh. Victor, her husband, had arrived ten minutes earlier and she was anxious to be off.

"It's such a long drive for him at the end of the day," she said by way of explaining her hurried departure, "and he *really* needs his evenings."

Her manner invited sympathetic agreement and Mr. Purdie made a murmured acknowledgement. Victor Morton, a quiet little dried-up prune of a man, smiled faintly. There was no need for him to make excuses when his wife was so vocal, and he did not mind it if she sometimes attributed to him what were really her own wishes.

"Come and see our lovely garden," said Aunt Isabel in farewell, "and we can really catch up on the news."

Together they melted into the darkness.

Father and daughter went into the living room. Alone with his daughter Mr. Purdie found impatience taking the upper hand, but he held it in check.

"Why did you leave home, Jane?" he asked mildly.

Jane hesitated. She had known this moment would come, but she could no more give an answer than she could have taken wings.

"What's been wrong, Jane?" Mr. Purdie rephrased his query.

Jane was silent in the face of his questioning, as she had been the night before with Aunt Grace. In this context, she reacted to interrogation as a rabbit in its burrow to a probing stick. It drove her deeper underground. Discontinue the effort and she would re-emerge.

Seeing that he was not meeting with success, Mr. Purdie then gave Jane an account of his own afternoon, concluding with a futile drive round the neighbourhood. Tears filled Jane's eyes but still she said nothing.

To the relief of both, Mrs. Oliphant's key was heard in the lock and Mr. Purdie rose to greet his sister-in-law.

"You'll stay and have a meal of course," she invited, brushing aside Mr. Purdie's excuses. "Walter will be in presently and he'll be disappointed if he doesn't see you."

She cast an inquisitorial glance in Jane's direction which told her absolutely nothing, but Mr. Purdie drew comfort from it. Despite the lapse of time since their last contact, his present need disposed him to have confidence in her, both as a woman and as an experienced social worker. He had never had much affection for either sister-in-law. Isabel was certainly more approachable but he thought perhaps that Grace was more reliable. She was after all a social worker.

With the arrival of Walter Oliphant, conversation became general. In contrast to his deep-thinking wife with her Freudian approach to life, Mr. Oliphant was agreeably ordinary and Mr. Purdie warmed to him over dinner. Aunt Grace did the honours in her usual commendable style and the meal progressed with something approaching conviviality.

At its conclusion Mrs. Oliphant drew her brother-in-law into the lounge.

"Walter will wash up—he's very good at it," she said with unconscious condescension as she switched on the gas fire, "and Jane will help him."

They sat down and Mrs. Oliphant turned her inquisitorial glance on Mr. Purdie.

"I believe congratulations are in order, George," she remarked, lighting the cigarette which he, as a non-smoker, had declined.

Mr. Purdie looked puzzled.

"I understand you're thinking of remarriage," she went on casually.

For a moment Mr. Purdie was speechless.

"Are you?" she pursued. "Forgive me for intruding in your private life, George, but this seems to be a matter of some importance to Jane."

Mr. Purdie seemed to be groping for words.

"To Jane!" he echoed in bewilderment. "What does she know about it?"

"More than you've been aware of, obviously," replied Mrs. Oliphant dryly, "and it's upset her. I think you've got some explaining to do—not to me, but to her."

Mr. Purdie was thunderstruck.

"Are you telling me, Grace," he asked, "that this is what has brought Jane here?"

"Exactly," nodded Mrs. Oliphant. "She was distressed on arrival but I could get nothing out of her. She told Isabel today and Isabel phoned me, in case there wasn't a suitable opportunity this evening for telling."

Mrs. Oliphant did not add that she had felt a little piqued that Jane had confided in her sister rather than in herself.

Mr. Purdie was silent. He needed time to assimilate the astounding news. It was his turn to feel something of a shock, with the realisation that his little girl had been adult enough to discern his attachment to Miss Chalmers. Yet, looking back over the course of the relationship—from the holiday at the Glen to his Friday evening meetings over the last few weeks—he could not see in what way he had betrayed himself. He felt embarrassed at the exposure of his own personal affairs, he who had acted so independently and responsibly since Elspeth's death. He even recognised a twinge of resentment against Jane, for having laid bare the details of his new joy to the two sisters who had never accepted him as a member of the family. Once again, he felt at a disadvantage but less keenly, with the confidence of maturity and experience, than in the days of his courtship. He swallowed his pride.

"What would you advise me to do?" he asked.

"You'll have to have a talk with Jane," said Mrs. Oliphant. "You must take her into your confidence, tell her exactly where matters stand. No more secrets. You don't want her to run away again, do you?"

***

The talk took place that evening as soon as father and daughter arrived home. The upheaval of the weekend's experiences demanded immediate action.

It was not easy. Jane froze at the outset. She was unable to raise her eyes to meet her father's and sat looking at the floor, shifting her slippered feet in meaningless formation on the carpet. Mr. Purdie was distressed but did his best to conceal his emotions. He reminded Jane of the strength of her own feelings for Miss Chalmers and appealed to her understanding in respect of his. He referred to the fortuitous meeting at the Glen, and the re-kindling of his emotions after initial encounters at the school; to his awareness of a growing reciprocal interest from Miss Chalmers and to their few outings since the late summer; to his confession of love and desire for marriage and his belief that in time this would in fact take place.

"I didn't at any point want to deceive you, Jane," he said in conclusion, "but I wanted to be sure of Miss Chalmers' feelings for me, before asking what yours were for her, not as your teacher, but as my wife."

Jane was silent. The pattern on the carpet was engrossing, with the toe of one foot she followed the outline of a floral motif, then repeated the action with the other foot.

"Perhaps this was wrong of me," mused Mr. Purdie. He was still suffering a reaction to the stress of the weekend.

Silence.

"What is it about my friendship with Miss Chalmers that's worrying you, Jane?" he asked.

But again, the rabbit was burrowing more deeply into its warren in terror of the pursuing stick. Confronted by her father's personal acknowledgement of his love, Jane knew a surging awareness of her proximity to a fire that blazed in terrifying splendour, and within which, like the comrades of Daniel, her father and Miss Chalmers walked unscathed, while she must retreat or be burned in the flames. His simple avowal, far from allaying her anxiety, served only to increase it, emphasising, as it did, the reality of a relationship for which Jane could find no place in her emotional life.

"I don't love you the less, Jane, because I love Miss Chalmers also," said Mr. Purdie. He had never seen Jane in this mood, though realising now that her taciturnity since the summer was but a prelude to the present development. In his own mind, he was groping for the words which would prove the key to the door of his daughter's personality, at present locked against him. This was the first and only break in their relationship and it grieved him.

"I know exactly what it is that made you love her so much," went on Mr. Purdie. "She's wonderful and beautiful just as you said, and if she agrees to marry me, I think we could all be happy together."

After a pause he added, "Don't you?"

At his words, it was as though the gates of heaven inched slowly open, and a beckoning finger invited the beggar outside to enter and share in the delights of the celestial pair. But the beggar was lame and could not even limp as far as the shining portals.

"Miss Chalmers has been just as concerned as I've been," said Mr. Purdie.

Jane looked up for the first time.

"Does she know?" she asked.

Mr. Purdie nodded.

"Yes," he said, "and that you're safe now."

It was a relief to see a reaction.

"She's a darling," he went on, "so kind, so anxious, and I love her very much."

His confession, complete in its simplicity, presented itself like the brief extracts of tomorrow night's film, intended, by their very incompleteness to titillate, to tantalise. In the words which were spoken, Jane heard only the echoes of overtones which were themselves too clamorous to be comprehensible.

Mr. Purdie was nonplussed. The complexities of his daughter's reactions to a relatively normal situation were beyond the understanding of a man whose adolescent problems had centred, like his mother's, on financial matters. Father and daughter sat in silence but it was not telepathy which eventually set Mr. Purdie's thoughts off on another tack. It had been a matter of concern to him, since Jane's twelfth birthday, that there was no woman relative sufficiently close to discuss with Jane matters which were of importance to her but in which he felt that he himself, as her father, could not intrude. Her questions from time to time had indicated her need for information, and his heart smote him now that he had not pursued the matter further, perhaps through Madge's mother.

He wondered to what extent the gaps in her knowledge were troubling her or if, indeed, the gaps had already been filled in such a way as to cause her distress. In shelving the matter before, he had vaguely decided that she would learn at school. Sex instruction was included in the curriculum nowadays, wasn't it? Or, was it?

Surely, Grace could be asked to help her. As a social worker, if not as an aunt, she might perhaps regard this as her province, especially as Jane herself had chosen to bring her back into their lives. Jane needed a woman. Who better than her mother's sister? If not Grace, then Isabel, to whom she had apparently spoken more freely.

There was Alison, of course. But even Mr. Purdie recognised that this was not a matter which could be referred to her.

Chapter XIII
Lunch With Aunt Grace

It was Saturday once more, Jane had had lunch with Aunt Grace and Uncle Walter. Mr. Purdie had not joined his sister-in-law for lunch but had left again after dropping Jane at her home. Jane knew where he was. He was seeing Miss Chalmers, but strangely enough, she no longer experienced the unspeakable agitation which had possessed her during recent months.

It had been a strange week. She had not been exactly happy, but, following on the crisis at the weekend, perhaps as a result of it, she experienced a welcome liberation from her anxieties. The situation had not altered a great deal except that Mr. Purdie had not kept his usual Friday appointment with Miss Chalmers, and, though its replacement with Saturday afternoon was no better in one sense, Jane knew, without having to be told, that the change was consequent on the previous weekend's happenings. She also sensed that today's outing was part of a plan and, with renewed trust in her father, she willingly agreed to visit her aunts.

But freedom from tension had been quickly followed by depression, because she was only too well aware that it had been paid for at a price—her father's distress; the forfeiture, if she had not already forfeited it, of Miss Chalmers' regard; to a lesser extent, that of her aunts. She had shown herself unable to cope with a fairly ordinary situation. Factors beyond her control had forced her to abdicate the throne of her own personality, and she was now in the ignoble situation of being propped in position, by hands that were either too loving or too dutiful to allow her to lie in the mud. For all this she was deeply ashamed.

But whereas stress had vanquished her utterly, shame and depression could be coped with. Already she felt new strength where before she had been perpetually drained by the stormy emotions which had pulled her this way and that. She might hold her head in shame figuratively speaking, but until last weekend she had been desensitised to every emotion other than fear and its ally, despair. But these had receded almost overnight and she could almost feel herself knitting together again. She began to feel that she was once more a person, even if that person was not a very happy one.

Nothing of a personal nature had passed between Miss Chalmers and herself. She had gone about her lessons with revived interest and a determination to make up for lost time. She no longer scrutinised Miss Chalmers' face or drifted away into an unhappy limbo of her own when she should have been paying attention. She did wonder, however, if her father had told Miss Chalmers why she had run away and what Miss Chalmers' reaction would be.

Lunch over, Uncle Walter set off for his golf club and Jane helped Aunt Grace clear up. She was sorry to see Uncle Walter go. He was pleasantly frank and uncomplicated compared with his lynx-eyed wife and he made Jane smile in spite of herself. In her imagination Jane saw her aunt as a sort of super electronic brain deriving its energy from a grid, which maintained a constant supply of power at peak level. The very stacking of the dishes appeared to be under its direct control, and Jane felt herself to be something of a favoured flunkey because she had been entrusted with the drying.

"Pile the soup cups here and the meat plates there," directed Aunt Grace in her acid voice. "Take your time, Jane. Be careful with each dish. The cutlery box is on the third shelf—knives, forks, spoons in separate compartments. Tea spoons at the side. That's the girl."

Jane felt a little nervous. Had she been in a brighter mood there might have been a degree of stimulation in following the instructions, just as she enjoyed exercising to numbers in the gymnasium.

"One, two, dry the plates. Three, four, lay them down," her aunt seemed to be saying. Her own deft actions as she washed and stacked were as precise as a machine, but Jane decided that the same sort of mechanised action was not her own forte and she decelerated in the interests of safety.

The soapy water swirled obediently away as Aunt Grace upturned the basin. With another dish-towel she helped Jane dry the remainder of the dishes. A quick wipe of the draining surface was followed by the whisking away of every plate in sight. Dexterity and speed appeared to be the order of the day.

Within minutes Jane and Aunt Grace were confronting each other from opposite sides of the fireplace in the lounge. Outside the evergreens were tossing restlessly in the wintry sunshine. Jane had been hoping that they would set out for Helensburgh immediately after lunch but Aunt Grace seemed to have other plans.

She lit a cigarette and inhaled in silence. Jane watched her apprehensively. Intuition told her that Aunt Grace was refuelling in preparation for some sort of an all-out offensive on herself. She wished vaguely that she too could be thus equipped and looked longingly at the still open packet of cigarettes on the occasional table beside Aunt Grace, which bristled belligerently as though it contained cartridges instead of cigarettes. Anxiety again took over.

"Your father asked me to speak to you, Jane," began Aunt Grace deliberately. "He's concerned over your anxiety about his friendship with Miss Chalmers and thought you might like to speak to me about it, perhaps to ask me if there was anything you did not understand."

She had decided on the direct approach. True, it had not worked the previous week but she felt on surer ground since Jane's disclosure to Isabel. Besides, the girl was her mother's double. *There* was a case where still waters had run deep, if you like. No one had ever understood Elspeth. The waters needed stirring.

"It's very sad to be without a mother at your age," she continued. "You're not a little girl any longer and there must be a great many matters you're wondering about."

She noticed Jane's averted eyes and sudden colour.

"It's not really so terrible if your father decides to remarry," went on Aunt Grace. "Mmm?"

Mrs. Oliphant was not altogether relaxed herself. She had agreed to help partly from a sense of duty, partly because she felt disturbed at her omission over the years to make contact with her niece, and she was now aware of how much she had missed. How much more easily she could have helped if a relationship had already been established.

"I've got a wee girl in a Children's Home at present, not so far off your age," pursued Aunt Grace, "who has been in care for three years because she lost her mother, and now that her father is going to remarry she's overjoyed because it means she can go home. Isn't it nice that your father was able to look after you himself?"

With this observation Mrs. Oliphant fell silent, but this time it was not the reflective pause of the thinker. The comparison of her niece with Kelly-Ann Quinn brought with it an abrupt reminder that the widowed Mr. Quinn's children had been received into care mainly because the relatives had declined to help. True, it was from Mr. Quinn's unfortunate addiction to drink that their disinclination to relieve him of his responsibilities had stemmed. But what would have happened to Jane if her brother-in-law had not been made of sterner stuff? Would she or Isabel have intervened? And yet, with all the disadvantages of institutional care, Kelly-Ann's outlook on life was certainly healthier than Jane's.

She lit another cigarette.

"I'm sure you remember how often your mother had to go into hospital," she said. "Do you know why?"

Jane sat through her aunt's interrogation as though turned to stone. Underneath her heart was racing and her head throbbing with an energy sufficient to have taken a rocket to the moon and back. She had advanced on legs which shook beneath her to remove the curtain which screened the mysteries of adult life from her view, but the desire to tear it open was countered by a psychic barrier which prevented her from stretching out a hand to reach it.

"Perhaps there's something you don't understand. There must be a great many things you're wondering about."

Aunt Grace's voice sounded seductively in her ears. With one part of her she wanted to scream, "Tell me, tell me!" With another she wanted to ward off the axe that was threatening her very life. Into what sort of a brave new world would she enter once the scales had dropped from her eyes?

She knew that with the knowledge, the gates would close forever on the childhood to which she clung as a preferable alternative to the unknown terrors of adolescence. Dorothy Reid and her friends had long since closed the gate. Miss Chalmers too. Aunt Grace was calling to her from the other side.

"Please tell me," she whispered.

***

It had not been easy. As an interview with a disturbed adolescent it was to stand out in Mrs. Oliphant's memory as few other interviews would. Accustomed as a social worker to live alongside the seamier side of life, Jane's ignorance had been something of a revelation to her in a decade where she had believed there were few secrets left. Teenage problems in Mrs. Oliphant's experience had tended to arise from a false set of values and precocious experiment rather than from a total absence of knowledge. Jane's inability to infer what Mrs. Oliphant thought was implicit in her carefully worded explanation had in fact caught her aunt off guard. Having led Jane gently but firmly along nine-tenths of what was to prove a precipitous path, she had not anticipated that the final step would prove such a stumbling-block. But here, Jane was unable to leap intuitively from the facts which were known to the central fact which was still unknown.

Aunt Grace emerged from the interview unwilling to recognise in her personal discomfiture her own failure to come to terms with this side of her marriage. How much easier it had been to warn the wayward girl against the risks of experimentation, than to impart facts which were to some extent almost as distasteful to herself as to her hearer, and to infuse into these facts a meaning and a glory which she herself had never found. Status and security she had known, yes. Intimacy and passion, no.

When the timid query came eventually at the end of a torrent of weeping, "Is it nice?" her answer was evasive, "For those who love it is."

As for Jane, she had at last crossed the line of demarcation between those who knew and those who did not, and had joined the company of the informed. She had eaten of the forbidden fruit and, by all the rules, now stood among the elect.

The tears of a lifetime, or so it seemed, flowed at last. The dam was opened and the waters rushed through with the force of Niagara. Her sense of decency affronted, her emotions outraged, Jane cried as she had never cried before. The disparity between her own idea of a spiritually determined pregnancy and the crude facts as outlined by Aunt Grace was more than she could assimilate, and she shrank in horror before this new concept of the source of life. The secret was a secret no longer. The loathsome facts dredged up from the turbid depths of the whirlpool by Dorothy Reid and her cronies had provoked in both her and them a strangely delighted reaction. They had sniggered and squealed with what now seemed perverted delight. Jane recoiled at the shamelessness of their attitude, but recoiled still further from the self who had now also penetrated the slimy profundities of the cesspool which was life, and had surfaced, besmirched, clutching her horrible find. Tainted by the same knowledge, she could no longer choose to be different from them. The door had slammed with a reverberating bang on an innocence which was irretrievably lost. Stunned by the undreamt of crudity of Aunt Grace's revelation, she groped helplessly for a new identity. No longer the child whose purity derived from ignorance, unable to accept the facts of adult experience, she was lost.

The implications of the newly acquired knowledge seemed in some respects to be even more horrifying. Wholly abhorrent to herself, this knowledge was obviously not only acceptable to others, but was translated willingly—indeed eagerly—into actual experience. Jane bowed her head as though in penance for the depravity of her sex.

But the facts would not stand still in theoretic isolation. The need to apply her staggering discovery to specific people of her acquaintance was strangely compelling—Madge's mother, whom she would have regarded as being above that sort of thing; Fiona's mother, whom she did not like so much, but even so... the mothers of all her friends. They all appeared in a new and unflattering light. For Mrs. Stephenson, it had been a twice round experience. For Mrs. Ross, three times. She thought of the families known to her and compared the number of children with her assessment—her former assessment—of the personality of the mother. It was a startling exercise. As for Mrs. McSporran! Jane shut her eyes.

Seeking desperately for some mitigating factor, she wondered if for some the implications of marriage had not been quite clear until it was too late to escape. They could not, like Selina McSporran, have experimented beforehand or marriage would certainly have been viewed with justifiable repugnance.

Aunt Grace herself. It was strange that she had not had children when she obviously knew what to do. Perhaps—she reverted to her former theory—it was because she had been too busy looking after other people's. But what about Aunt Isabel? Could it be that, like herself, she had regarded this function with distaste and had therefore refrained? In that case, she had surely taken a great risk in getting married, thereby putting herself in such a vulnerable position. But perhaps Uncle Victor did not like it either.

Then there were the countless millions since the beginning of time, who would never have been born if other people had only had the sense to reject this fleshly means of procreation as she now did. Did she alone have a vision sufficiently clear to perceive the essential rottenness of the system? She wept afresh. Surely, God in His omnipotence could have chosen some other way.

But a deeper trauma still was to ravage her sensibilities when her thoughts turned, as they inevitably had to turn, to her parents. The mother whose memory was hallowed and who, above all women, had provided Jane with a standard of selfless devotion, now stood defiled in her daughter's sight. Not once but five times she had demeaned herself. Her father? No, on his role, social taboo forbade her to dwell.

But to acknowledge the foulness of their act was to negate the validity of her own being. The bonds between her parents' union and her own life were inextricably mingled. The abomination of their iniquity rested not only on herself but also on the lives of her four little unborn brothers and sisters whose memory was so precious to her. Perhaps, indeed, it would have been better if neither she nor they had ever been born, if the world had terminated before it was begun. Whence came the immortal soul if derived from such earthy origins? Surely, even the desire for babies should have shrivelled before the ordeal which was to be endured before conception could occur.

And Miss Chalmers? Was this the experience which she and her father sought to share? The idea was insupportable. Her anguish sought to express itself in indignation. Surely someone could explain to them that love was possible, was much nicer, if not polluted by this unwholesome activity. If her father married Miss Chalmers, would they want a baby so much that they too would be willing to break through the barriers of common decency? Perhaps her father would be so afraid of losing more babies that they would decide to conduct themselves with the propriety befitting sensible people.

As her sobs quietened, giving way to a series of breathless shudders, Jane wondered if Aunt Grace had perhaps made a mistake. It was inconceivable that such a peculiar exercise should always be in process of performance somewhere, without someone wanting to report on it. Why had she not heard of it before?

Forgetful of her cigarette, Aunt Grace had watched the convulsive sobbing of her niece and had felt strangely helpless. Tears in plenty she had seen but there had always been a remedy, either from her own personal stock of wisdom or with reference to a specialist in another field. Efficient and benign as she had been, her work was based on the belief that within the State system existed the remedy for every ill. The subconscious dynamic of her own life lay in the conviction that the caseworker was clever and the client was clay. When the facts did not fit her theories, she tended to shut her eyes to them. This time, however, her own particular problem had risen up fairly and squarely in the distress of her niece. For once the electronic brain had ceased to function.

She was glad Walter was not there, even in the next room, to be aware of Jane's anguish. She wished it was time for George to come back. It was planned that they should, all three, go to Helensburgh for their evening meal but given Jane's distress, this now seemed out of the question. Isabel was the last person in the world whom she wanted to see at that moment. Isabel, she suspected, could see through the role of the busy busy social worker and it was important for her at the moment to continue to play it. George, in his own need, would require her to play it, so George would be a support. The sobs had subsided and only by an occasional moan did Jane betray the travail of her soul.

"I think we could do with a cup of tea, Jane," she concluded. "I'll put the kettle on and you can go and wash your face."

***

Alison sat with George at lunch in the Pantry, a centrally situated restaurant which was busy enough at midday on a Saturday to afford privacy to its patrons. The couple at the corner table needed it. The events of the previous weekend had rocked the boat in which they had been cruising so delightfully. For George, the tempest had been totally unexpected. For Alison, the storm clouds had already appeared on the horizon but action had been inappropriate. Someone else had held the oars. She had turned her back on the clouds when George proposed marriage. The sky in front had been a rapturous blue.

The following day, with the news of Jane's disappearance, they had gathered menacingly above her head. The relief on hearing of her pupil's safe arrival in Paisley had been of short duration and was quickly replaced by the certainty that the storm was about to break. George's refusal to discuss on the telephone the source of his daughter's anxiety was confirmation enough that it centred on their friendship. The substitution of Saturday for Friday evening was a further indication of her own involvement.

There was nothing in Jane's bearing during the week to allay her fears. Her own Achilles' heel pierced, she found the carefully husbanded strength of recent years draining rapidly away. She was already geared for the severing of her friendship with George before Saturday came.

He broke the news to her very gently but it was clear that he did not fully understand her dread of a situation in which rejection seemed implicit.

"Jane's finding it difficult to accept my friendship with you, Alison," he said. "Grace is going to have a talk with her this afternoon. She can do this better than I can. I'm sure it will all work out."

But Alison did not share his optimism. The anxiety which had engulfed Jane had now settled on herself. Her end of the seesaw was hurtling downward into the trough while Jane's, she supposed, was lifting correspondingly.

George did not see it like that. There was no question of polarisation. The seesaw might at the moment be a little uneven but he had no doubt that the balance would shortly be restored.

"Jane likes you so much," he argued. "This is why I feel sure that it's really something else that's bothering her, something connected with the situation and yet not connected with it, if you follow."

His innate good taste forbade him from further detail.

Alison looked down at her plate. She had ordered a snack only, and even for this she had little appetite.

Memories of Alastair and Hector came crowding back into her mind. With the stability of recent years, she had forgotten what pain felt like. She had grown away from her dependency needs. She had matured. She had deemed herself impervious. Anticipated rejection now brought in its train a repetition of the experience from which her whole being shrank. Alastair had rejected her in favour of another woman. Hector had courted her while choosing to remain married. George had a daughter who could not accept her father's love for her. The wounds which she had imagined healed opened afresh. Once more she was undergoing the trauma of former years, so unspeakable in its intensity that it blotted out everything else.

She reviewed the events of the last few months—the casual contacts with Jane's father which had developed so quickly into something deeper, and she wondered helplessly how she could have allowed it to happen in the face of the danger signals sounded by the wiser—or more frightened—part of her personality. She appeared to have learned nothing from experience and was no more able to cope with an emotionally explosive situation now, than ten years previously.

"Jane will come round, you'll see," said George reassuringly. "Grace will help. Probably Isabel too. We'll have to keep in touch with them now that Jane has dug them out."

Alison shook her head. She was very near to tears.

"I'm sorry, George," she said quietly but with a firmness which startled him. "I can't go on with it."

George stared.

"I don't understand any more than you do why Jane has been so upset," said Alison, "but I think it's—it's unwise for us to continue seeing each other."

George was aghast. He attempted to take her hand which lay slightly clenched on the table, but she withdrew it hastily. A tear coursed down her cheek.

"Please, George," she whispered, "don't make it difficult for me."

But George was so bewildered by her unexpected decision that he needed to question it. The waitress approached and he asked for the bill.

"Look here, Alison, we can't speak properly in this place," he said. "Let's go for a spin and we can have some fresh air on the subject."

Alison shook her head. Her feelings for George were very deep but her defences were up and she could maintain them only so long as they were not alone.

"But, Alison, I just don't understand," he protested. "Jane's going through a phase. She'll grow out of it. It's just a matter of time."

Another tear ran down her cheek. The paper napkin which she had been twisting nervously was beginning to disintegrate.

"Yes, Jane needs time, George," she replied, "time to grow, to develop, to come to terms with life. And while she's doing just that, she must not feel the need to look over her shoulder to see how you and I are shaping up. She must be free to take a step forward into maturity, without the fear that *her* move will be followed by one from *me*."

It was an effort to say this but she knew that what she said was right. For herself, there was no other path.

Her words fell on incredulous ears.

"Alison, my dear, my dearest girl," said George earnestly and with rising emotion, "let me say with all the sincerity at my command that I love you more than ever for your understanding. But if you withdraw, don't you see, you're taking away the very situation that Jane needs for her growth."

He sighed reflectively.

"I daresay we've been too close, just the two of us. I've been all she has had, just as she has been all that I had. Without you, we'll be back to square one again."

He took her hand and this time she did not withdraw it. He longed to kiss her.

"Alison, dearest, we both need you."

His argument on Jane's behalf was plausible, her own need for him very real, his for her. Possibly Jane's need for her also in spite of the psychic barrier that she had raised between them.

Her hopes for the future were cruelly dashed. Somewhere there was an intangible element in Jane which was blocking the way, but it would take a more secure personality than she was to identify and remedy it, while maintaining a relationship with her father. She was only too well aware of her limitations. If Jane needed help, it was not her role to give it.

Perhaps, too, there was a degree of pride which she acknowledged as an ingredient of her personal insecurity, and without which she would have been able to function more effectively. She would not, could not, seek Jane's confidence to further her own ends. That the motherless girl had deep emotional needs she had always recognised, but the clash with her own needs in this particular situation could not be set on one side, and for the sake of her own emotional integrity her withdrawal from the situation was vital. It was with a heavy sigh that she acknowledged the expedient and not the solution in her decision.

Chapter XIV
An Afternoon With The McSporrans And A Visit To Another Purdie Family

Jane surveyed the living room of Mrs. McSporran's home with interest. There being no telephone, she had cycled the short distance from her own home on an errand from her father. It was her first visit and she had been anxious to see the matriarchal dwelling.

Having brought up their own brood in a two-room and kitchen tenement flat, Mrs. McSporran and her husband now found themselves the proud occupiers of a four-apartment house in a new housing area. With only themselves and three small foster-children to fill it, they had initially felt themselves lost in what seemed like limitless space. The strangeness, however, had quickly evaporated in the pleasure of decorating and furnishing. A timely win on the pools precipitated a snap decision to scrap the accumulated conjugal furniture and to start afresh. Complete therefore with colour telly, deep freeze, fitted carpets and new suites for each room, they took possession of their dream home. The glory of their wedding day was a pale counterpart to the éclat with which they launched the new domestic craft. For Mrs. McSporran, life began anew in her middle fifties.

She took Jane round the house.

"I got the colour telly for the weans," she explained.

A film of the week's sport was showing, viewed so intently by Mr. McSporran that he had not apparently noticed Jane's arrival. He was a short, skinny little man with lank, well-oiled hair plastered back from his brow. Made redundant from a local foundry some twelve months after their occupancy, he had since divided his attention between the new television set and his football coupons, on the intricacies of which latter activity he spent considerable time, his ambition being nothing less than the jackpot.

Jane looked at him curiously. It seemed strange that a potent personality like Mrs. McSporran should be dependent for completion on such an insignificant-looking little man.

The three foster-children, two boys and a girl, together with two of Mrs. McSporran's grandchildren, played contentedly on the floor, oblivious of the coloured glories which had been intended for their edification, but which more frequently commanded the rapt attention of the man of the house.

The youngest McLuckie, recumbent and unconscious in his pram, had also been entrusted to Granny for the afternoon while Jenny and her husband went round the Barrows. In addition, Selina's baby was being minded while Selina 'helped out' at the Supermarket where her mother, Mrs. McSporran's youngest daughter, was in full-time employment.

On the rug, in front of the fireguard lay Whisky, the McSporrans' mongrel. In the kitchen was closeted Whisky's daughter, Soda, Selina's mother's pet, in view of the uncertain feeling which existed between the two.

"It's ma autumn room," said Mrs. McSporran, pointing from the rust and yellow foliage of the carpet to a similar leafy pattern on both the suite and the wall. But for the television, the visitor might indeed feel as though they had stepped into a wood in October.

"Ma best bedroom's rosepink," went on Mrs. McSporran, leading the way upstairs. From fitted wardrobe to satin headboard, its trendiness was beyond question. Her mind temporarily monopolised by the information imparted by Aunt Grace, Jane however found her attention irresistibly drawn to the conjugal bed which dominated the room, and her imagination exercised itself in a fashion which was now becoming habitual. The result was still one of astonished incredulity.

"The boyses' bedroom's lemon," continued Mrs. McSporran, opening the second door on a room containing a set of bunk beds with sunny coverlets. "They're aye arguin' aboot who's tae sleep in the top bunk. Ah tellt them it wis to be week aboot, but see that wee Alec—he'll be seven at his birthday—he'd start a fight in an empty hoose."

They went into the third bedroom which was Patsy's.

"Ah done it in lilac," said Mrs. McSporran proudly. "See her wee suite—I pickt it oot a catalogue."

The neat little bed, together with miniature wardrobe and dressing-table in this tiny boxroom of a bedroom, was reminiscent of a large doll's house.

Jane was enchanted but wistful too. She would have liked this little room for herself, with her brothers next door scrapping for supremacy. She admired Mrs. McSporran's expressive choice of words—rosepink, lilac, lemon. She could almost smell the fragrance of the first two, almost behold the luscious fullness of the third as it ripened under a Mediterranean sun.

"She didnae like a bedroom tae hersel' at first," went on Mrs. McSporran. "She said it was too quiet and she couldnae sleep."

She laughed.

"She's that auld-fashiont. I think she missed the boys—they a' slep' in the wan room where they came fae."

The bathroom, complete with shower, was in lime-green, the kitchen sky-blue. There was something of the poetess as well as the artist in Mrs. McSporran. The common or garden adjective was not good enough when it came to describing the appurtenances of her palatial new establishment.

Downstairs, Alec and Hughie, on all fours, travelled miles over the warm foliaceous pile, in pursuit of their bools. The ten-year-old David, a quieter child except when Alec sought to outpace him, had withdrawn from the game and now squatted at Mr. McSporran's feet, alternately cuddling and wrestling with his legs. At the far end of the room, Patsy and Hughie's big sister Linda, were in a world of their own. A doll's tea set provided the focal point of their fantasy, with a newly acquired toy telephone placed inappropriately beside the teapot on one of a nest of tables.

"They're a' that different," said Mrs. McSporran emotionally. "But I love them a'. Naebody knows what thae wee weans means tae me. Mind you, I'm no sayin' I don't lose patience with them at times. See if I wis a teacher! I'd get hung. It's no that I've no got the brains tae be a teacher, I've no got the temperament. But see that man!"

She indicated the silent Mr. McSporran with a nod of the head. "He's the best man that ever walked the face of this earth. And patience!"

Words failed her to describe the monumental attributes of her spouse.

"He never lifts a haun to them," she continued. "Of course, he never lifted a haun tae his ain."

She sighed.

"He left a' that tae me."

She turned to wee Hughie with a word of reproof.

"Gonie no dae that, son."

Wee Hughie was picking his nose.

An argument broke out between the two sportsmen on the floor regarding the respective ownership of two almost identical marbles, and as the argument developed into a scramble for possession, two heads cracked resoundingly together. There was a resultant howl from Hughie who immediately sought consolation at his granny's knee. Alec rubbed his head ruefully but was more concerned with arbitration than comfort.

"Whit's a' the fuss aboot, take wan each," pronounced the descendent of Solomon, gently rubbing the head of the afflicted Hughie.

"Alec'll never greet in a fight," said Mrs. McSporran, turning to Jane. "An' see his heid! You'd break your knuckles on it—it's like the road."

David, observing that the activity of the room was centring, as it not infrequently did, on Mrs. McSporran, relaxed his hold on Mr. McSporran's legs and sidled over. He was a serious boy with a good-sized head and slow, deliberate speech.

"This is David," said Mrs. McSporran proudly, rumpling his hair. "He's a very affectionate boy. What are you going to be when you grow up, David?"

She knew what his ambition was, but wanted to put the children through their paces for Jane's benefit.

David turned his big slow eyes in Jane's direction.

"I'm going to be a footballer," he replied, "then I can make a lot of money for ma mammie and ma daddie."

Jane felt very shy. She knew that some sort of delighted reaction was expected of her but she could not think what to say.

The question was put to Alec who had already forgotten his sore head and was restlessly looking round for an alternative activity.

"I'm going to join the polis," he replied with a grin.

"The polis run a club for boys up at the cross every Friday," added Mrs. McSporran by way of commentary. "David goes tae. He wantit tae learn the bagpipes but he's no got the puff."

Then, it was Patsy's turn. She looked up from her teapot and her telephone.

"Ah'm goin' tae be a mairrit wumman," she announced.

Mrs. McSporran laughed her toothless laugh.

"She's that auld-fashiont!" she repeated.

Jane was abashed. The child was six years her junior, but in her naive practicality she appeared already to have travelled safely and securely across the line.

"Come and read tae your mammy," said Mrs. McSporran persuasively.

Patsy, ever willing to display her talents, eagerly produced a reading-book from a miniature schoolbag and opened it with great ceremony. Very much aware that the spotlight was upon her, she set the marker meticulously in position, made as though to start, then changed her mind and laid the book on the floor in order to smooth her hair back. Positioning herself for the second time, she looked to Mrs. McSporran as though for reassurance but really as an excuse to put the fussy little question,

"Will I do the new bit?"

Mrs. McSporran looked over her shoulder.

"Was that the bit you got the sweetie for?"

Patsy nodded. This was what she had wanted her foster-mother to say.

"Begin a page or two back, hen, that bit's awfy short."

Then followed more play-acting and hair-smoothing, until Mrs. McSporran had been cajoled into agreeing with Patsy on the appropriate page.

Patsy was the best reader in her class. She aimed to please, kept her voice well up, giving equal emphasis to every syllable of every word. From one page to the next and the next again, she continued while the assembled children listened with due respect. Even Mr. McSporran transferred his attention. Baby McLuckie dropped off. Only her arrival at the frontiers of the unknown brought the performance to a halt, and the actress retired to the wings with the triumph of a prima donna.

"See ma man!" exclaimed Mrs. McSporran, still beaming with satisfaction at such a display of virtuosity. "He idolises that child. He thinks as much of her as he did of his ain."

David was gaining confidence.

"Ma mammie and ma daddie are going to buy a car with their Spot-the-Ball money," he volunteered. This was a Saturday competition in the local paper.

Jane, who had hardly uttered a word since her arrival, managed to find her tongue at last.

"That's very nice," she said shyly.

David hastened to rectify her apparent misunderstanding.

"They havenae won it yet but," he said honestly.

At that point Selina's baby, who had been essaying for some time to add her voice to the assembly, now decided to give a full demonstration of lung power. As though by arrangement, Baby McLuckie also chose that moment to express his need for attention. Not to be outdone, Whisky shook himself out of his somnolence and added his contribution. In echo, Soda yelped from the kitchen.

The silent Mr. McSporran rose mechanically from his chair, glided across the leafy carpet and lifted Selina's baby.

"She's soakin'," he said.

Mrs. McSporran lifted the youngest McLuckie. He too had wet his nappy. Wee Hughie was still hiccupping between his sobs and, having been rejected by his Granny in favour of the baby, stumbled with renewed howls, towards the ladies in the corner in search of further sympathy.

Jane did not know where to look and would gladly have fled the field. She had never before been present at a nappy-changing session, and to find herself the observer of a double act created a paralysing sense of embarrassment. She wondered vaguely about the propriety of Mr. McSporran's handling of a female infant but, glancing over, she noticed that he seemed perfectly at home with the operation, whisking the baby deftly from one position to the next, dexterously applying the powder and attaching a snowy-white nappy in position with a practised hand. Strange that each parent should pick up a baby of the opposite sex. Or had they simply taken the one that was nearest?

Meantime, Mrs. McSporran was keeping up an affectionate monologue in a language which the youngest McLuckie seemed to understand.

"He's saying thank you for the nice clean nappy, is that no right, son?" she said, tickling the baby's chin so that he smiled back at her with a smile as toothless as her own. 'Ta!' he says, she repeated with another tickle. 'Ta!'

"Cheeky boy! Where's the wee smiles? Oh, there they are!" she cried with delight, when another ghost of a smile lit up the baby's face, accompanied by further contented noises.

"He says he loves his granny and it's time for a wee cuddle," explained Mrs. McSporran, immediately complying with the request as interpreted by herself.

In the corner, wee Hughie had now joined the ladies' tea-party. Selina's baby had fallen asleep in Mr. McSporran's arms and he had renewed his interrupted viewing. David had joined Alec on the floor with the marbles.

Jane wondered curiously where David, Alec and Patsy had come from. Once again, the newly acquired knowledge thrust itself on her attention and she concluded that somewhere along the line, a mistake had been made in their procreation. Certainly, they had not dropped from the skies. Somehow or other, they had made a forced entry into a world which was not ready for them and the cause of their arrival was this incredible urge of two people of opposite sexes.

She gazed at them wonderingly. They looked like any other children and despite the error of their conception, they seemed happier than Jane knew herself to be.

"Their ma and their da have split up," explained Mrs. McSporran as though reading her thoughts. "He promised her heaven an' he gave her hell. He gave her a bunch o' fives on the kisser. He's lyin' in Barlinnie the noo an' their mammy's away wi' another fella."

It was all so different from her own quiet home. The house was teaming, bubbling, surging with life. Dogs and babies had contributed to the joyful abandon of the atmosphere. Compared with what now seemed the rather torpid stream of her own life, here was a river in full spate, running exultantly from its source to join the sea. There was no place in this turbulent onrush for either linguistic or mathematical mysteries, which roused so much pleasure in the tortuous recesses of Jane's mind. There was an elemental quality in Mrs. McSporran's way of life which brought Jane face to face with the very stuff of which life was made.

Back at home was her father, grave and kind, his vision once more circumscribed by his work, his home and his daughter. He had told Jane, without a word of reproach, that he would not be seeing Miss Chalmers again because neither of them wanted to cause her further distress, and Jane had accepted the news with ambivalent emotions. With her visit to Mrs. McSporran's home, she was dimly aware that she had deflected the flow of two streams which, united, could have formed a current as tumultuous and jubilant as that which she was now witnessing.

The sadness induced by such reflections all but overwhelmed her. But not quite, because at the back of it all stood the psychic barrier which she had found insurmountable. Much as she longed to plunge into the maelstrom of life, the hurdle on the riverbank was too high and justified her retreat.

***

"Come away in," said Uncle Robert. Aunt Ina echoed his welcome and Mr. Purdie and Jane stepped across the threshold of the family's council dwelling. It was the first reunion between the two brothers for over three years and George, aware of his own tendency to isolationism, knew that he was going to be slow to respond to the easy geniality of his brother and sister-in-law.

Robert had been the youngest of the Purdie family and had been largely protected from the financial stresses and strains through the efforts of his older brothers and sisters as, one by one, they entered employment. There had consequently always been something of a barrier between himself and George who, as the eldest, had borne the brunt of the family's responsibilities.

Not only had his childhood been easier. His adult life had run more smoothly. Without his brother's ambition to join the ranks of the white-collar workers, Robert had taken up an electrician's apprenticeship on leaving school and in recent years had built up a business of his own. Ina, from a similar working-class background as himself, had made him an excellent wife and now helped in the running of his business. There were three children—two daughters and a son, the elder girl being a year older than Jane.

The girls had only the slightest recollection of each other and exchanged uncertain smiles. Sandra was taller than her cousin and altogether more grown-up. Where the child of former years was still discernible in Jane, the young woman of the future was very much in evidence in Sandra. She attended teenage discos at the local community centre, had her bedroom walls covered with pictures of the latest pop stars and had been fashion conscious for some time.

Jane looked at the platform shoes, the calf-length skirt and the hair that grew down past her shoulders. Conscious of the maturity conferred on her by her twelve months' seniority, Sandra surveyed the sober-looking Jane with her knee length socks, flat heels and short skirt. She had heard a great deal about her clever cousin at Earlswood but was clearly disappointed in what she saw. A spontaneous mutual antipathy developed. Jane very quickly sensed the difference in their respective levels of maturity, and unerringly placed her cousin among those for whom the crossing of the line had presented no great difficulty. Such she regarded as enemies of their own sex.

Doreen, at eleven, presented no such threat to Jane's timid approach to womanhood and she therefore felt more at ease with her younger cousin.

Bobby, a sturdy eight-year-old, was so much like his father and therefore like her own father, that Jane immediately recognised in him her pretend-brother, young Robert. She felt a great glow of happiness and returned his friendly grin as though she had known him all her life.

The family took their seats round the table and Aunt Ina served the steak and kidney pie through the hatch. The two brothers sat at either end and Jane was delighted to find herself between Doreen and Bobby. Sandra sat opposite and was later joined by her mother.

Bobby gave her a poke.

"We're cousins," he said.

Jane beamed. Cousins! She belonged!

"Stick in till you stick out," Uncle Robert exhorted them jovially.

Sandra frowned.

"Stop trying to be funny, Dad," she remonstrated.

George smiled faintly. He remembered with dislike his younger brother's forced witticisms of former years. It was all very well for him! He pulled himself up. No, this sort of attitude would not do. He had deliberately sought out Robert and his family for Jane's sake. He must try to cultivate a more charitable attitude.

"That's a delicious pie, Ina," he commented.

Aunt Ina smilingly waved aside his appreciation.

"I always like to make something special for them at the weekend," she replied. "They all come and go at different times during the week. It's really only on Saturday and Sunday that we can all sit down together."

Uncle Robert outlined the week's schedule.

"Doreen and Bobby have the first sitting, Sandra the second," he explained. "I can come in at any time."

Sandra took up the tale.

"Dad's nearly always late at night," she said, "Bobby's got the cubs on a Friday at six o'clock, Doreen's got her dancing class on Monday at five and I go swimming with Christine on Wednesdays at six."

Jane was impressed. With two members of the family missing, there could still be three at the table. She made a mental count of the present company. Seven, and they all bore the same surname!

Aunt Ina had watched her as her eye travelled round the group.

"Are we all present, Jane?" she asked.

Jane nodded.

"We're all Purdies!" she replied.

She showed a healthy appreciation of the meal and won Aunt Ina's heart by accepting a second helping. Sandra, on the other hand, straightened her knife and fork when she was only half way through the plate.

"What's the matter with you?" demanded Uncle Robert.

"Nothing's the matter," replied Sandra sulkily. "I just don't want it."

"Don't force her, Robert," intervened Aunt Ina. "You know she doesn't have a big appetite and perhaps I put too much on her plate."

"I don't know what's come over her recently," said Uncle Robert. "We put good meat on the table and she won't eat. Is it still this slimming craze?"

Sandra flushed and her mother flew to her rescue once more.

"Leave her alone, Robert," she urged. "She's going through a phrase."

Jane's eyes met her father's and she knew that he too had noted the intrusive 'r'.

Jane had always cleared her plate, partly because she enjoyed her food and partly because, at an early age, she had been taught that this was the best way of expressing appreciation for the culinary efforts of a mother who was so often unwell.

"Thank you for a lovely meal, Aunt Ina," she said at the end of the meal. This too she had learned to say from early childhood.

Aunt Ina, whose own children were much more casual in their eating habits, was more surprised than gratified by her appreciation. She took it for granted that there would always be some item that was not to someone's taste or mood.

"Take Jane into the bedroom and you can play your records," said Aunt Ina, having declined Jane's offer of help with the washing-up. "No, hen, never mind. It's not often we see you and your Dad and we don't want to spend the time over the sink. Sandra'll help me later."

Sandra and Doreen occupied twin divan beds in the second bedroom, each adorned with spotlessly clean pink nylon coverlets. A woolly dog, as clean and new as though purchased that morning, lay propped against the pillow of each bed. On the chest of drawers sat a row of colourfully arrayed dolls.

"This is my bed," announced Doreen, indicating the one nearest the door. "And this is Fi-fi."

She lifted the soft toy and cuddled it.

"Sandra's is called Lu-lu. They're our watch-dogs. Sandra's sits on her bedside table to see that nobody comes in but I take Fi-fi to bed with me."

Jane could not but register surprise at learning that a woolly toy and dolls could still bring pleasure to the grown-up Sandra, even to the eleven-year-old Doreen. She herself had long since discarded playthings such as these.

She looked round the room. The bedroom furniture was painted white with gold handles and a portable television set stood on top of the chest of drawers. Each girl had a small transistor and, next to the wardrobe stood a record cabinet with a record-player on top. From the walls, a host of current pop idols alternately leered and smirked at their fans, each picture displaying to advantage the chief attraction of its subject, from massive shoulders to narrow hips, from hairy torso to ocular blankness, each face remarkable only for its complete and utter inanity.

"Who's your favourite pop singer?" asked Sandra.

Jane was nonplussed. Her father had nothing but contempt for this new aristocracy and the idolatry it had created. She accepted his viewpoint for the most part without question, but was anxious not to give offence to her cousin.

"It's difficult to say," she replied evasively.

"I like Larrie Cox but Darren Blyth's Sandra's favourite," Doreen piped up. "Look, there he is over there above her bed. She kisses him every night."

From beneath a tangled halo of curls, his eyelids drooping sleepily, Sandra's idol appeared to be extending a frankly seductive invitation from the coloured cut-out. Sandra bridled.

"Well, you're just as crazy about Larrie Cox," she countered. "Look, you've got him all over your side of the room."

Sure enough, there was the youthful Larrie, smiling so guilelessly as he twanged his guitar, clutched his microphone and posed on his motorbike, that you could be forgiven for believing in his integrity.

Jane hastened to pour oil on troubled waters.

"Are these your records?" she asked shyly.

Sandra invited her to examine them, meanwhile putting on her most recent purchase. A series of bangs and catcalls proceeded from the record-player, but there was just sufficient recognisable evidence of a beat to set Sandra swaying where she stood, a faraway look in her eyes.

Jane looked in vain for something familiar in this legion of apparently identical discs whose titles, one and all, seemed to indicate that the singer was in the last stages of survival.

"What records have you got?" asked Doreen.

Jane had been given a record-player the previous Christmas and had already collected half a dozen records—some Strauss waltzes, selections from the Savoy operas, Scottish Country Dances and the odd classic that had captured her interest.

Sandra made no comment. She wanted clever Jane to see that *she* belonged to a world where things happened. For Doreen, however, the mention of Scottish Country Dances had some significance.

"I go to Highland dancing," she said eagerly. "I can do the Highland Fling and the Sword Dance and the Sailor's Hornpipe. Do you want to see?"

She fumbled for the appropriate records and eventually put one on, though not without opposition from Sandra who considered them out of date.

The sound of the pipes quickly brought Uncle Robert from the living room. He was proud of his younger daughter's accomplishment and anxious that his brother should witness her performance.

"She's won cups galore," he announced proudly. "Ina, get them out and let George and Jane see them. Her teacher's putting her in for some of the Highland Games next year."

The table was pushed back and Doreen gave a graceful performance, her expression alternating appealingly between gravity and vivacity. There were records enough to allow her to give several selections from her repertoire. Both George and Jane were wholehearted in their applause.

"Come and see my bedroom," clamoured Bobby who had been feeling outnumbered.

Unmistakeably a boy's room, there were model aeroplanes suspended from the ceiling at all sorts of interesting angles, pictures of footballers on the wall, a dartboard with a protective surround, a transistor, even an action man on top of the tallboy.

Jane's bedroom was simply a bedroom. It contained the essentials and there were one or two pictures of her own choosing. While murmuring his appreciation, Mr. Purdie found the opulence of the girls' room and the respective masculine and feminine elements distasteful. He had, of course, seen this modern decorative trend before in varying degrees, and it had always struck him as representing an adult's conception of a child's bedroom rather than the spontaneous choice of the child himself.

The sound of the ding-dong bell brought a delighted exclamation from Uncle Robert.

"That's Anne and Tommy," he said. "We told them you were coming and they said they'd be over."

Anne was George's younger sister and Tommy was her husband. As was the case with Robert and Ina, Mr. Purdie had not met them for some years and he made some show of pleasure at the reunion.

Annie, as he had known her, had always been a rather colourless young woman who had lacked personal initiative, but who had nevertheless been endowed with some indefinable capacity to extract attention from others. He had never liked Tommy, an aggressive little runt of a man, whom she had married on the rebound, and who had an irritating need to over-compensate for his mediocrity. George was surprised to see what nice-looking lads—ten and twelve—they had managed to produce.

"Great to see you, George," said Tommy, clasping his brother-in-law's hand in both his own. "Hullo, doll," he greeted Jane. "Meet your Uncle Tommy."

He doffed his sheepskin motor-coat with a flourish.

"And where's my beautiful niece?"

Sandra simpered, recognising the compliment for herself.

Tommy's artificially curled hair clung crisply to his neck above the figured collar. A hacking jacket and flared trousers completed a rigout which would more appropriately have dressed a younger man.

"Anne, this is George's girl," said Uncle Robert, putting an affectionate arm round Jane's shoulder.

Anne's lips made a big round O as she gasped her surprise at the difference in Jane since she had last seen her. Aunt Annie's heart was in the right place but her frank appraisal of her niece was felt by Jane to be embarrassing. She wore a perfectly tailored costume which showed her slim figure to advantage.

James and Ian smiled shyly to their new cousin.

"And where have you been all these years, George?" asked Tommy, removing the cellophane from a packet of cigarettes and offering them to his brother-in-law.

George declined and Robert and Tommy lit up. Aunt Annie offered Aunt Ina a cigarette. All four inhaled.

"Oh, the usual round," replied George casually. "The days are pretty full and I like to put my feet up at night."

"We were at Majorca for wur holidays, isn't that right, Anne?" said Tommy, stretching back in his chair. "Luxury hotel, private bathroom, private beach, sun from morning till night. Oh boy, oh boy!"

He puffed reminiscently. George knew what was coming—a minute-by-minute account of his holiday in the sun which would put the travel agent's brochure to shame. In spite of his resolve to be cordial, he knew he must endeavour to cut him short.

"I think we ourselves had the weather of the century in Scotland this year," he commented. "We were in our caravan as usual, Jane and I."

He would have preferred to give a wide berth to the subject of holidays, but it seemed impossible.

Uncle Tommy stared.

"Away!" he exclaimed incredulously. "A do-it-yourself holiday, eh?"

He put a hand in his trouser pocket and the jingling of coins was heard.

"That wouldn't do for us, George," he replied with irritating condescension. "Me and Anne and the boys like to have it on a plate when it comes to wur holidays. I mean, we work hard all the year, and I think we deserve a good holiday."

"Well, it makes a wee change," said Aunt Annie with undeniable triteness, "and it's an education for the boys."

Somehow or other the evening passed, but Mr. Purdie had his eye on the clock. He endeavoured, within the limits of courtesy, to curb his brother-in-law's eloquence but ultimately gave up, unable to compete with the encouragement he received from his wife and the more tolerant attitude of Robert and Ina. Halfway through the evening, Robert produced a bottle of whisky which had a lubricating effect on Tommy's vocal cords. The children were despatched to the girls' bedroom with crisps and ginger. Minutes later, a cacophony of sound proclaimed that Sandra's latest record was once more in rotation.

Chapter XV
Hope For The Future

Time rolled past with the blind deliberation of a driverless bulldozer in low gear, flattening alike the rough places and the structures which had been so hopefully erected. One aching heart viewed the straightening road with the numbness which comes when pain has been relieved by anaesthesia. Two others viewed it with an agony akin to bereavement. For all three, life continued outwardly as though nothing had happened. The suppressive influence of daily routine forbade the outward show of loss. Inwardly, the mind oozed an eternal interrogative to which there appeared to be no answer.

Mr. Purdie was no stranger to misfortune. He had already faced it in the loss of four babies and in the ultimate loss of a dearly loved wife. He had experienced the loneliness of a man who has domestic responsibility but is unsustained by domestic comfort. This he had coped with, finding strength in the very responsibility which denied him freedom. He had shouldered more than his share of the blame for Elspeth's death—it had been so hard to refuse her eager desire for children. He too had wanted a family. Four times, happiness had been almost within their grasp before the final calamity had overtaken them. Now, under totally different circumstances, it had happened again. Because the blow had not fallen with the same apparent finality, Mr. Purdie had not at first believed that the new love which had given him new hope was to be withdrawn with the decisiveness of death itself. He knew of the broken engagement and the subsequent romance, and, confident in the strength of his own love, had foreseen no barrier to a happy outcome, other than Alison's possible failure to reciprocate his feelings.

He had been as mystified at the decisiveness with which she had withdrawn as at the crisis in Jane's reaction to their association. To himself as the man in the middle the problem did not exist, or, if it did, it was of modifiable proportions. To find the same unyielding quality in his usually tractable daughter and in the woman who was so sweetly and irresistibly lovable, was to create a bewilderment so complete, that it effectively delayed his assimilation of the new situation. He had sensed from the first that time was an important factor for Alison in her acceptance of him as a husband. He had never imagined that Jane too might need time. On Alison's assessment, however, no term could be set on this need, and she had therefore vanished, wraith-like, from his life. He had telephoned and had been requested not to with what he felt was undeserved abruptness. He had written and received a brief reply in the same tenor. He had questioned Jane and found himself confronted by a stone wall. His initial belief in a mutual settlement underwent a slow but inevitable change until at last he retreated baffled, with an acceptance of defeat that all but stopped up his lifeblood.

Not until he had fallen in love with Alison had he realised to the full the isolation of the last five years and the limitations which it had imposed on his inner life. He had a deep capacity for emotion, but only with its re-awakening had he become aware of the extent to which it had shrivelled. His horizons had suddenly widened. New love had brought new life which pushed back the confining daily routines and opened up limitless possibilities. The finite quality of daily experience assumed the mantle of the infinite. He had reached the frontiers of eternity. His own personality had merged with a wider life, and he rejoiced in the everlasting affirmative which he now felt in very truth to be at the centre of the universe.

He believed that in due course Alison would marry him and there would be new joy in his domestic life. The gap which both he and Jane had grown to accept without question would be filled in the most delightful fashion. The need which both had ceased to recognise would be acknowledged only with its disappearance.

Once more the household would be at full strength. Perhaps there would be children. He knew how much Jane had wanted companionship in the home. He remembered her distress after the third miscarriage.

"If I can't have a wee brother, I want a wee dog," she had cried, but there could be no question, either at that time or following Elspeth's death, of adding to the household.

Strengthened with this new vitality, he felt ready to overcome any obstacle. Any obstacle but the loss of love itself.

To feel the walls of a restricted life again closing in on him was to look on spiritual death. He sought to stave off the shrinking horizons which he beheld advancing on all sides. He struggled to prop up the tottering structure of his life with the delusion that all would yet be well.

To accept what seemed inevitable would bring a sort of peace. This he knew. But for the time being, it was beyond his capacity to re-enter the narrow existence of recent years. It was he who now needed time—time in which to learn to renounce hope, to readjust to the norm of contracted living, to lose sight of the conception of ecstasy.

In the travail of his spirit he faced the impossible—he must detach from all that was best in himself if life were to become bearable. He must take leave of the element which was as vital to his soul as the air he breathed.

***

For Miss Chalmers, life had become an escape from she knew not what. Her step quickened, her voice sharpened, her every movement suggested a readiness for immediate flight. The brusqueness of her manner prohibited inquiry. Her family read the signs and mourned for her in silence, aware that sympathy would be rejected. She confided in no one, nursing her aching heart to herself. Only in bed did she allow herself the solace of tears. Again and again, she asked herself helplessly how she could have permitted herself to become engulfed in the emotional whirlpool which for her seemed destined to have one ending only.

Self-defence prompted the panic-stricken retreat from her friendship with George Purdie. She recognised only too well the integrity which, given the need for choice, would bring him down, at whatever personal cost, on the side of the daughter to whom his loyalty was already pledged. Twice she had been rejected. This time she would anticipate the decision and herself instigate renunciation.

The distraction which on another occasion had been provided by her work failed her at this juncture. Each day in five the child who she knew had loved her so deeply sat silently before her in class, unidentifiable from her peers in her school blouse and tie, but recalling by her very presence the relationship which might have been, and thus the man who would have created that relationship between them.

***

For Jane, the weeks following that unforgettable half-term holiday represented a period of bewilderment during which she vibrated between home and school with the automatic motion of a pendulum. There was the unspeakable relief of the termination of her father's relationship with Miss Chalmers. She knew that she could trust him when he told her that it was finished. But with relief came an oppressive sense of guilt over his sacrifice on her behalf. Then too, looming largely in her mind, were the disclosures made by Aunt Grace. Over these she brooded at first with incredulity, then with the passive acceptance of a mind rendered torpid by months of strain.

Unlike Miss Chalmers, she found consolation in the daily contact as though drawing comfort from the fact that she had not utterly destroyed her rival. As one of thirty pupils in the class, she enjoyed the protection of numbers denied Miss Chalmers. Only when singled out to recite or to answer a question did she experience an embarrassing awareness of their conflicting interests, but she only had to recall her own acute unhappiness in order to stifle her feelings of guilt. She would also justify her dearly bought security with reference to the fleshly lusts which lurked even within someone so apparently pure and lovely as Miss Chalmers and which certainly required punishment.

As the weeks passed, she emerged slowly but inevitably from limbo-land. The balance of her thinking, which had been disproportionately weighted by conflict and trauma, was gradually restored. The world around her resumed its former reality and once again her friends were relegated to their accustomed rank in her affections.

Though far from being her former buoyant self, she found an equilibrium which enabled her to meet the challenge of each day. Occasionally, she scrutinised her father's plain, beloved features which had worn a new gravity in recent weeks. She knew only too well what had caused this and deliberately averted her eyes, forcing herself to think of something else. The intimacy was missing from their relationship. The daily confidences ceased. Something important was lost. The spontaneity dropped out of the mutual interaction of their personalities. The silences which had been an acceptable part of life between two persons of widely differing age groups, now assumed an unwelcome significance. She wanted to throw herself into her father's arms and cry from her sorrowful heart, "Oh Daddy, please forgive me!" But the factors which had prevented her from allowing him a love life of his own, now sealed her lips and she looked the other way.

She had also noted the change in Miss Chalmers, as had some of the other girls.

"She jumps on you for nothing at all," commented Fiona.

"She's not as nice as she used to be," put in Madge.

Angela Brown's speculation was nearer the mark.

"Perhaps she's been crossed in love," she suggested.

Jane said nothing. They were arranging their books for afternoon classes.

"Do you still love her as much as you used to?" asked Madge.

Jane paused only for a moment.

"Of course I do," she replied.

And so she did. With the recession of anxiety, the energy which had fed it flowed again along its accustomed channels. She looked again with softened heart on the face that her father too had loved, listened again to the voice which had brought her so much delight, and wished with all her soul that she could make Miss Chalmers happy again. But it was not within her power.

Like them, she wondered sadly where life was leading her. The satisfactions which she had found in school and home, the two poles of her existence, had crumbled and she looked in vain for a substitute. Neither Aunt Isabel nor Aunt Grace could provide it. Nor could Uncle Robert nor Auntie Ina. She had nothing in common with Sandra. James and Ian as yet seemed unlikely companions. However congenial they had seemed, they were, after all, boys and she wasn't used to boys. Doreen and wee Bobby were much more likeable. She hoped to see more of them but, even so, they were but fellow pilgrims on the road, while the real object of her quest was the very nature and goal of the pilgrimage itself. She had never before stopped to consider life from this angle. She had just got on with it. Perhaps it was only when you were unhappy that you had to ask what it was all about.

***

Founders' Day. The end of January. The short days just beginning to lengthen. An occasional suspicion that spring might once again shed its benign influence. Activity at the school. In the anti-climax of the days following the Christmas holidays, the girls eagerly accepted the challenge of rehearsals for the musical performance traditionally held. Throughout January the sound of solos, duets and choruses, of piano, violin and orchestra echoed and re-echoed in the early twilight. Girls sang and girls played, girls chattered, girls whispered, girls laughed and were happy. A time, like many others, to be remembered.

It was an afternoon gathering and was followed by a buffet supper in the dining hall. Governors and principal members of staff occupied the platform, the latter resplendent in hood and gown.

There were speeches, reminiscent and eulogistic. The concert items were described as indicative of the school's current vigour. Reference was made to recent successes by former pupils at University, at colleges and in their respective careers. Compliments were paid to the continuing excellence of the staff and to the academic standards which they upheld. In the flowering of their womanhood, the girls could find no finer examples than in the dedicated women who taught them day by day. The youngest pupil presented a bouquet to the chairman's wife with a well-rehearsed curtsey which brought benevolent smiles to most faces.

Loud cheers greeted all remarks. Parents and pupils permitted their enthusiasm full rein. Staff beamed or smiled modestly according to their respective temperaments. On an occasion such as this, even the weariest decided that it had been worth the effort.

The school chaplain gave a short address. He led the school in prayer. An unseen choir provided the Amen.

Miss Marshall sat at the organ, specially tuned for the occasion. The Twenty-third Psalm was sung by all present.

In his rich, sonorous tones the chaplain gave a final reading from the Scriptures.

"When thou passest through the waters, I will be with thee; and through the rivers, they shall not overflow thee; when thou walkest through the fire, thou shalt not be burned; neither shall the flame kindle upon thee."

The organ purred quietly in prolongation of the serious tone which the chaplain's words had evoked. A few heads bowed uncertainly. Tears sprang unbidden to the eyes of a man, a woman and a child in all that great gathering.

In what secret fashion was the truth wrapped away? Or was it true?

The benediction followed. Then came a respectful silence while the good man resumed his seat.

Tongues broke loose.

"What a splendid programme!"

"How well Celia plays!"

"That was Joan in the front row of the choir."

"I hear the buffet's always delicious."

One parent slipped quietly away.

***

Freed from the crippling tension of former weeks, Jane was able to thrust her unhappiness on one side so far as her schoolwork was concerned, and once more her performance improved. Hostility and fear were replaced by compassion and a strong desire for a restoration to Miss Chalmers' favour.

She was aware of the change in Miss Chalmers and felt deeply unhappy about it. It was impossible not to notice the unaccustomed asperity that had crept into her tone and the occasional forced smile which had nothing of warmth in it. Once again, she was conscious of the great gulf yawning between them and of the apparent hopelessness of the situation. Whereas she had recently regarded Miss Chalmers as her own particular bad fairy, she now felt that there had been a reversal of roles, and this caused her to recoil as though she had seen a leprous reflection of herself in the mirror. Small wonder that Miss Chalmers should preside at her desk as from a wintry throne, her expression glacial, her voice cold. In imagination, Jane saw her wreathed round by a frame of icicles which so chilled the surrounding atmosphere that the prospective suppliant shrivelled at the mere thought of an approach. Where was the spontaneous good humour, the personality that had been warm as a summer's day, the dancing eyes of girlhood that had lingered into maturity? Jane thought of the sunny waters of Loch Darroch. Did they too now lie bleak and frozen, ringed round by a protective circle of snowy peaks? Cruel-lovely, in Jane's eyes the most beautiful person who had ever breathed, while she herself was the Jonah whose sacrifice to the waves would spell survival for the ship.

In private, she wrote a number of pathetic little letters in which she begged for forgiveness, but these were consigned to the flames. A personal approach was out of the question. Sometimes, she toyed with the idea of simulating a collapse in class, which she hoped would be recognised by Miss Chalmers as symbolic of inner torment. As she gradually regained consciousness, she would falter a few broken words of contrition which would bring tears to Miss Chalmers' eyes, and the relationship would be restored. As enacted in Jane's imagination, this was a very moving scene. In the cold light of day, however, common sense prevailed and she recognised the impossibility of staging her little drama.

It was Friday afternoon. The bell had rung.

Jane's face wore a grave expression, which was surprising in view of the good mark she had received. The class dispersed but Jane seemed intent on packing and repacking her books, eventually assuming a motionless pose at her desk.

Miss Chalmers eyed Jane narrowly for a few moments. Obviously, having assumed the pose of a tragedy queen, she was now expecting a response. Had circumstances been normal she would have made some cheerful comment on the laggardness of her pupil. The silence became deafening and once more Miss Chalmers hardened her heart.

"Goodnight, Jane," she said shortly and crossed to the door.

There was no reply from the statuesque figure. No matter. The play-acting, which she knew was for her benefit, would terminate as soon as the actress realised that her audience had departed. She left the room and made for the staff-room at the end of the corridor, disturbed in spite of herself. In order to justify her action, she reminded herself of the many buffets which she herself had been dealt by fate. Thus bolstered in her attitude, she continued on her way. She refused to be manipulated. Life had taught her a stoic's philosophy, the comfort of which lay in the tenet that all things, good and bad, ultimately pass away.

"This too will pass," she had affirmed, sometimes in resignation, sometimes in despair. And it had, carrying with it a part of herself. The amputation had been severe and the wound had never really healed.

Impossible to pass on such a comfortless philosophy to someone only just emerging from childhood. It was an expedient, not a solution. Nor would she be so hypocritical as to murmur some sort of over-the-counter pleasantry, or to select from her store of wisdom, the appropriate anodyne to be applied as deftly as a piece of sticking plaster. In front of the staff-room she paused, unable to forget the motionless figure that she had left behind with uncharacteristic lack of concern. The door opened and the dignified Miss Kelvin, in coat and hat, emerged. The older woman noticed her indecision.

"Well, Miss Chalmers, are you coming or going?" she asked cheerfully.

Coming or going? It was months since she had known. She smiled faintly.

"I've left something behind in the classroom," she replied mechanically and turned on her heel. She did not know what she intended doing or saying. That she would find the pose abandoned, she did not doubt and she was therefore surprised—and unexpectedly touched—to find Jane where she had left her, her desk still littered, the contents of her bag still on the floor.

With a slow yet sudden glimmer of insight, she found herself reaching out unaccountably to give welcome to a reality in which, like an echo from the unknown, she apprehended pain as well as pleasure, shade as well as light, each an inseparable part of the whole. Like the coming of dawn, understanding broke upon her consciousness, bringing with it illumination and healing.

Till now she had elected to identify only with what the world called the positive aspect of reality. Could it be that love was deeper and wider than that which she had channelled so carefully into her relationship with Alastair and Hector and George? That, born of a willing acceptance of suffering, it could be channelled anew to a needy world awaiting the enrichment which was hers to give and to receive in return.

She did not need to look beyond Jane.

"Tell me all about it," she said.

***

Jane had nothing to say, at first, retreating into her customary shell. But when a hand touched her cheek, she found a more satisfactory medium of expression in tears, tears which flowed in a strange blend of misery and joy, and which brought an unspeakable sense of liberation because offered to someone whom the weeper loved.

The hand, soft and smooth, was stroking her cheek and gently pushing back the hair which straggled across her face. Jane did not remember having experienced anything quite so delightful. She wanted to look up and smile through her tears at the owner of the hand, but chose to make no response lest the caress should cease.

Nor had Miss Chalmers much to say either. She sat down at an adjoining desk so that she might be nearer to Jane, and when Jane fell on her knees before her she held her face in both hands so that they became wet with her tears. A great silence fell on them both, broken only by an occasional sigh from Jane.

Past and future ceased to exist. Lifted up into an eternal present, Jane found herself sustained and restored and healed. The scattered fragments of her personality knit together and the disintegrated psyche assimilated the long-lost element which it needed for completion. The corner-stone was restored. The missing link endowed the chain with the strength it lacked. The mother, who had withdrawn as an effective force from the daughter's life long before death claimed her, lived again. As for Christian at the gates of the Celestial City, it was as though a great burden had rolled from her back, leaving her free and unconstricted, as though newborn.

She had wept to Aunt Grace whom she had not loved and who had ignored her emotions.

Aunt Isabel had stroked the hair from her brow but, like her sister, had not been able to reach out to the hunger within her.

Nor had Uncle Robert or Aunt Ina or Auntie Anne.

Mrs. McSporran, more than any of them, seemed to have discovered the art of living but she, Jane felt intuitively, had needed no guidelines and had therefore none to pass on.

But here, with her head cushioned on Miss Chalmers' knee, was acceptance at every level. Without a word being spoken, communication in its deepest sense had passed from one to the other. For the woman, it signified an advance from the limitations of her own personality, an advance which had led her from the confines of self-pity to comfort the one who had impeded her own quest for completion.

For the girl, it was the fulfilment of a search which had started in early childhood. A new concept of womanhood crept into her consciousness. She had found a new ideal with which to identify, an ideal which extended far beyond the performance on the hockey-pitch or on the water-skis, beyond the academic qualifications and the ability of the teacher. It was that of the essential woman with her capacity to accept and comfort and cuddle, yes, whether it be child or man.

***

It was after five when they rose to their feet. Miss Chalmers gave Jane's shoulders a squeeze.

"I'll run you home," she said.

*****

The car drew up outside the Purdies' home where a light in the hall indicated that George Purdie had already arrived.

Jane gathered up her possessions, her heart was filled with a strange new warmth.

"Thank you for the lift," she said. "But I'm sure Daddy will want to thank you too. Would you not like to come in?"